Madness
AT
Moonshiner's Bay

Children's Books by
Sigmund Brouwer

FROM BETHANY HOUSE PUBLISHERS

www.coolreading.com

Accidental
DETECTIVES

Madness at Moonshiner's Bay

SIGMUND BROUWER

BETHANYHOUSE

MINNEAPOLIS, MINNESOTA

Madness at Moonshiner's Bay
Copyright © 2003
Sigmund Brouwer

Cover illustration by Chris Ellison
Cover design by Lookout Design Group, Inc.

Published by Bethany House Publishers
11400 Hampshire Avenue South
Bloomington, Minnesota 55438
www.bethanyhouse.com

Bethany House Publishers is a Division of
Baker Book House Company, Grand Rapids, Michigan.

Printed in the United States of America

Library of Congress Cataloging-in-Publication Data

Brouwer, Sigmund, 1959–
   Madness at Moonshiner's Bay / by Sigmund Brouwer.
      p.   cm. — (Accidental detectives)
Summary: While vacationing in Florida, twelve-year-old Ricky Kidd and his friends get caught in the crossfire of a family feud involving moonshine, a missing fortune, and murder.
   ISBN 0-7642-2571-5 (pbk.)
   [1. Mystery and detective stories. 2. Christian life—Fiction. 3. Florida—Fiction.]
I. Title. II. Series: Brouwer, Sigmund, 1959–   . Accidental detectives.
   PZ7.B79984Mad   2003
   [Fic]—dc22   2003014706

SIGMUND BROUWER is the award-winning author of scores of books. He speaks to kids around the continent in an effort to instill good reading and writing habits in the next generation. Sigmund and his wife, Cindy Morgan, divide their time between Tennessee and Alberta, Canada.

For Olivia
and the sunshine you bring
into this world

You have to wonder about the sanity of a kid who decides to share a Disney World dream vacation with his three favorite caterpillars and a battered old teddy bear.

Unfortunately, I didn't notice those caterpillars until they were cruising at six hundred miles per hour along with the rest of us on our flight to Orlando, in central Florida.

"Joel!" I don't know how many times I've had to hiss that name in a low whisper.

He raised his eyebrows in hurt shock. He's had practice at that, of course.

Joel is my six-year-old brother, and he haunts me worse than any ghost. I'm twelve, but he terrifies me. Somehow he appears and disappears when I least expect or want it. Walls and locked doors don't stop that kid. When I do spot him—which is rare— he says nothing, only stares at me with solemn eyes that take in exactly whatever I'm doing at that moment, which usually happens to be something I want nobody in the world to see. Then, as I'm bursting out of my skin with terror at his sudden appearance, he's gone again.

That's why I had breathed a sigh of relief to see our seating arrangements on the plane. It was a full flight, and since none of us had been able to sit together, Joel was to the left of me— across the aisle and firmly and safely wedged between two large grown-ups.

I had the aisle seat on my side, with an old lady and her husband on my right. The old lady's hat was so wide that I could barely turn my head to look across her out the window. Other than that, it was a good seat. Far enough away from Joel for freedom, close enough to watch him. The rest of our group—Lisa Higgins, Mike Andrews, and Ralphy Zee—were scattered throughout the plane.

But now as I looked over at Joel, I stifled a groan. Joel was still playing with the jam jar he must have somehow smuggled onto the plane. The jar contained a few leaves, some stems of grass, and, of course, his three favorite caterpillars.

Great.

"Joel!"

I couldn't hiss too loud. The guy immediately to my left, in the opposite aisle seat—directly between Joel and me—sat with his chin slumped into his chest. Asleep. And he didn't look like the kind of guy you wanted to wake.

He was so big that his knees crammed upward between him and the seat in front. All I could see in profile was his huge wedge of a nose and the way it hung over a thick and drooping walrus mustache.

"Joel!"

It didn't work. Joel smiled, shrugged, and held his jar in front of him, admiring his friends inside. He set the jar sideways and shook it, just to make the caterpillars topple over each other and fight for balance.

"You look nervous, sonny. Scared of flying?"

I jumped an inch off my seat at the unexpected voice in my ear. *Even away from me, Joel still finds a way to scare me.*

"No," I replied to the old lady on my right as soon as I could breathe. "It's just that ... that ..."

How do you explain Joel to someone who doesn't know about him? Especially since he had just tucked the jam jar out of sight.

"Yes?" she asked, wrinkles squinted in question marks.

Change of subject needed.

"It's only an hour before we land," I said, giving her my full attention. "Will you be visiting Disney World?"

Her puzzled frown broke into a delighted beam of false teeth as she nodded proudly. "Our first time," she said, pointing at her husband in the window seat beside her. "We've heard so much about it from our grandchildren that we absolutely had to see it for ourselves."

I smiled with her. Disney World was the perfect way to end our summer vacation. Our gang had waited forever for this!

To pass time, I explained to the lady how we'd helped a movie star named Jericho Stone get rid of blackmailers and how he'd decided to reward us with this trip. How it nearly looked like the trip would be canceled because of some business stuff involving my dad. How at the last minute my parents had decided to send us ahead and catch up in a few days with my baby sister, Rachel. How it had been arranged for someone to be waiting for us to help us out for those few days until our parents arrived. How—

Joel!

From the corner of my eye, I saw what I didn't want to see. Joel was unscrewing the lid of his jar.

I froze.

The old lady's husband asked her a question, and she turned to him, which left me alone and helpless to stop Joel.

I glared at him. He smiled again, shrugged again, and lifted the lid clear of the jar.

I raised my top lip in a silent snarl. He pouted but did not replace the lid.

I clenched a fist and slowly raised it in his direction. That actually worked. Joel began to move the lid back to the top of the jar.

And the plane hit a pocket of turbulent air and bounced down. Only half a foot. But that was enough.

I think it was the surprise of that slight drop. Joel overreacted as he juggled the jar. The rest seemed to happen in slow motion.

Joel's eyes widened in surprise. His hands popped upward. And leaves and caterpillars shot from the open mouth of the jar.

I groaned.

The old lady beside me asked for the napkin on my lunch tray.

"My husband just spilled his coffee," she explained. "Turbulence." As if I didn't know.

I barely remember handing her the napkin because my eyes were riveted on the upcoming disaster.

One of Joel's caterpillars—naturally, the biggest and greenest one—had landed on the big man who was still asleep in the aisle seat between us. Not only that, it landed on the man's right shoulder. Out of Joel's sight and out of Joel's reach.

"Joel!" I hissed yet again.

He ignored me in a frantic search to recover the other two caterpillars. The third one inched toward the big man's neck.

It about killed me.

One monstrously sized man in a dark suit so old it was back in fashion again. One huge green caterpillar creeping onto a shoulder so big it strained against the threads of that suit. And me, the only person aware.

I mentally screamed at the caterpillar to reverse direction and head back down. No surprise, that effort didn't work.

The old lady beside me fussed over her husband's shirt front. *As if that's the most important crisis!*

My blood slowly turned into lumps of fear. The caterpillar made a determined march onto the man's thick neck. The man twitched slightly and grunted but did not wake.

I knew I didn't have much time. Joel was too busy searching for the other caterpillars, and this one was rapidly getting within range of that slicked-down mustache.

All I could think of doing was to grab the in-flight airline magazine. *Maybe I can just roll it into a baton and—*

I gasped. The caterpillar was already on the man's broad cheek and racing for his mustache, the closest thing it had seen to a leafy branch since leaving home.

I would have to reach over with my rolled-up magazine and flick the caterpillar away with the utmost speed . . . and with enough delicacy not to hit the man's face.

Without daring to stop and wonder at my craziness, I reached across the aisle. I brought back the magazine to give a quick flick and—the huge man woke just as the caterpillar explored the hairs of his right nostril.

I tried stopping my swing, but it was too late. The man had jerked forward in surprise as he woke. My gentle flick became a solid blow across the man's nose and forehead.

He opened his mouth to roar outrage, and the caterpillar dropped inside. The man clamped his mouth shut in surprise.

So far everything had happened in silence. The next moments were no exception.

His eyes popped wide. We stared at each other. Then, slowly, I dropped my eyes to look down at the man's lap, where half a caterpillar squiggled its yellow guts onto the dark fabric of the man's suit.

He followed my eyes downward. Then turned a chalky white. It didn't take a genius to guess the location of the other half of the caterpillar.

I did the only thing possible. I offered the man my airsick bag.

CHAPTER 2

I expected those giant, gnarled hands to form themselves into grappling hooks that would reach across the aisle and squeeze my throat into a toothpick.

Instead, the big man accepted the airsick bag, brought it up to his chin, bowed his head, and quietly dropped the half caterpillar inside. He folded the bag neatly and handed it back.

In return, I gave him the half can of Coke left on my tray.

He took a mouthful, swished once before swallowing, and drained the rest in three gulps.

"Thanks, son," he said in a voice that sounded like one boulder grinding against another.

I started to try to explain. "It was crawling on your face, sir. I thought I'd be able to—"

That's when Joel tapped him on the leg and began a quiet question. "Have you seen—hey!"

Mournful indignation and accusation filled Joel's face as he, too, saw only half a caterpillar.

"He's dead!" Joel lifted his jar to show the other two caterpillars inside. "What am I going to tell his friends?"

The man turned to me and raised his eyebrows in question.

"My brother, sir," I said across the aisle.

The man nodded, then bent his head and spoke in a low voice to Joel.

The constant and muted roar of jet engines that filled the

airplane cabin made it impossible to overhear their conversation. When the huge man first spoke, his tone sounded apologetic, as if he was sorry for causing grief in the lives of the other two caterpillars. Then it became more animated, with both Joel and the man nodding and gesturing with their hands.

Of course I was curious.

Joel only speaks about two words a year. He's more into silent terror. Yet here he was, gabbing like my dad's friends in front of a television and Monday Night Football.

The high pitch of the jet engines dropped as the airplane began to descend. The man looked up briefly, then went right back to his discussion with Joel.

For the last half hour of the trip, I alternated between dreams of excitement in Disney World and amazement at the contrast of those two across the aisle. A kid with a teddy bear and a jar of caterpillars. And a giant with fists like sledgehammers.

They spoke until the plane finally rolled to a stop at the terminal. As the plane emptied and it was our row's turn to leave, the big man let me move into the crowded aisle first. When he stood, his shoulders almost hit the luggage compartments.

Joel must have made a good impression, because the man reached down and shoved one of those massive hands in my direction. I tried not to wince at his powerful grip as we shook hands.

"The name's Clem Pickett," he drawled. "I'd be pleased if y'awl would let me give you and yo' brother assistance with yo' luggage."

Like I was going to argue?

The big man waited at the gate with Joel for Mike and Lisa and Ralphy to join us before walking ahead to show us the way.

I answered Mike's shrug with a whisper. "He wants to help. Would you disagree?"

Mike grinned no.

"Besides," I said, "the chauffeur will be waiting for us at the luggage carousel."

Mike grinned a crooked grin again. "Chauffeur ... limousine ... Disney World. We're gonna be stars!"

"Dream on," Lisa told him.

They, too, made quite a contrast.

Mike Andrews. Freckles. Red hair. Perpetual New York Yankees baseball cap. A grin to charm chocolate chip cookies from the grumpiest of old ladies. Mismatched sneakers. And a constant itch to try the impossible.

If Mike was fire, Lisa Higgins was a cool breeze. Long dark hair, and eyes the color of a clear September sky. She's twelve, like the rest of us, and doesn't have to be a tiny ghost like Joel to drive us nuts. She has a smile of sunshine that makes you want to stare but also a scowl of thunder that makes you want to run.

Worse, she's good at sports. What she can't do, she'll practice until she can. Once Mike teased her about throwing like a girl. She spent two months every day after school pitching a baseball into the playground backstop until she could wing it so hard that the next time Mike caught one from her it sprained two of his fingers.

That left—behind us and trailing slowly—Ralphy Zee, computer genius and even more of a bookworm than I am.

I slowed as Mike and Lisa bickered and continued to follow Joel and the huge man.

"That's one of the people who got on the flight during our stopover in New York, right?" Ralphy asked when he caught up.

"Yup," I said, then passed on the only information about Clem Pickett he had told me while we left the plane. "He's from some place up there with a weird name. Sing Sing, I think."

"S-sing Sing?" Ralphy stuttered.

"Yup, I thought it was strange, too. You'd figure with an accent like his, he'd be born in Georgia or Florida."

"You're not going to like this," Ralphy said. I shouldn't have been surprised that he knew enough to explain what he did. Ralphy is a walking book of information. "Sing Sing is not a town. It's near a village called Ossining. The village changed its name because it didn't want to be known for Sing Sing."

"Huh?" I said. "What's Sing Sing and why wouldn't the village want—"

"Sing Sing is a prison," Ralphy said. "It's one of the biggest in the country."

CHAPTER  3

I sputtered, but not from disbelief. Ralphy has a set of encyclopedias where most people just have brains.

"The guy's an ex-con?"

Ralphy nodded.

Wonderful.

"An ex-con," I repeated. Clem Pickett and Joel were ready to board the shuttle that would take us from the terminal to the main building of the Orlando airport. Clem waited by the open door and waved us forward.

As Ralphy and I hurried ahead, I spoke from the side of my mouth. "I guess we'd better make sure Joel goes easy on the poor guy."

Sometimes it's money—finding out a person's rich. Sometimes it's what someone's parents do for a living. But have you ever noticed how once you know something about someone you look at that person differently?

It shouldn't work that way. If you figure that a certain kid is a jerk and then find out his dad owns a baseball team, suddenly you might decide the kid is just a guy who jokes around a little too much. Or you figure someone else is cool; then someone tells you his dad just declared bankruptcy, and without even trying to find out if that's true or not, you suddenly think that kid's someone who tries too hard to say and do the right things.

It shouldn't happen that way. But it does.

Hard as I tried to fight it, it was difficult now to see Clem Pickett as only a big, quiet man who had been gentle and helpful with a kid who wasn't happy about losing a third of his caterpillar collection in one unfortunate bite.

Clem Pickett *did* seem different.

Now—in the nearly empty shuttle to the main terminal—his quietness had become the brooding of a hardened criminal. His pale skin was not the natural color of someone who worked in an office all day but that of someone who had spent years in darkness. The ragged hair was not someone three weeks late to the barber but someone who never needed to care about appearances. Those giant hands that gripped and dwarfed the handrail were maybe the hands that had held a gun in an armed robbery. Those . . .

He caught me checking him over.

I quickly looked down. But not before I saw in his eyes a deep sadness.

I looked up again. Clem's eyes were still upon me. He opened his mouth as if to say something, then shut it again as the shuttle slowed.

"Orlando, here we come!" Mike said. He didn't wait for us to agree or follow. He just bolted for the stairs below the sign that pointed us down to the luggage carousels.

Lisa went next, purse swaying at her side as she managed to keep up with Mike's pace and somehow still look considerably more dignified.

Ralphy moved ahead of me. As usual, too much of his hair stood straight up, and his wrinkled and overly large shirt was untucked, which made him look thinner than he was. Mike always says that Ralphy's so skinny he has to run around in the shower to get wet.

Joel and I were behind Clem as he disembarked from the shuttle.

He stopped briefly as if checking both ways for traffic, like someone afraid of crowds. Then I kicked myself mentally for imagining too much. *Just because he's fresh out of prison doesn't mean he's nervous in a public place.*

Clem ambled ahead.

My first move was to try to grab Joel's teddy bear—a battered brown creature with gray-white paws, which serves as his security blanket. It was my only guarantee that Joel would remain at my side instead of disappearing. Joel, however, gripped the bear tightly and stuck close to Clem. I decided to just keep a close eye on him instead.

All of us arrived at the carousel as the conveyor belt started to spit luggage free.

Then I felt a hand on my shoulder.

I jumped, a natural reaction after years around someone as quiet as Joel.

"Ricky Kidd?"

I turned, and all I saw were the brass buttons of a chauffeur's uniform.

"Hello, sir," I said, more on instinct than thought.

"Sir? Not me. I'm the one hired by Jericho Stone to escort you and your friends for the next few days."

My ears turned red. "You're a, I mean, it's just that . . ."

She sighed. "That I'm a she. So I'd appreciate no woman driver jokes."

Her grin showed that she didn't mean it. I barely had time to step back and look up into her face before a shout interrupted anything else she might have to say.

"Hey, you!"

That brought most of the buzz of nearby people to a dead silence. The luggage belt clunked on, and suitcases thumped in rhythm.

"That's right. Freeze!"

Two cops were headed straight for us at a half run.

I didn't have to turn to see who they meant.

Clem's drawl reached all of us clearly. "Relax, boys, it ain't nothing to get your britches in a knot."

As if it were just him and Joel alone in the middle of a deserted field, Clem squatted to his knees and looked Joel square in the face.

The cops were less than twenty yards away and not slowing at all.

"Take care, son," Clem said gravely to Joel. "You've been a big help."

With that, Clem shook Joel's hand good-bye. Then he straightened and shook my hand and winked a friendly wink, as if cops with hand-cuffs flashing shiny and ready were nothing out of the ordinary.

Clem faced them, stuck his hands out, and offered his wrists to the first cop, a shorter man with greasy skin and a patch of white hair as obvious as a lightning bolt in the dark of the rest of his hair.

Clem spoke first. "I reckoned he might send someone to git me outter here. Not that I'm real pleased to see y'awl."

CHAPTER 4

"I don't know why we need a hotel," Mike said from his corner of the backseat of the limousine. "There's enough room in here for a couple of beds and *another* television."

He was nearly right. Outside, I knew, was the wall of heat of a Florida afternoon. But inside the limo, cool air poured over us as we waited in front of our hotel while our chauffeur, Amanda—who had smiled and explained that "Ms. Amanda Elaine Suzanne Carmichael" was much too long and awkward—made arrangements at the front desk for our rooms.

The limo stretched so much that it held *two* backseats—a regular one facing forward and another facing backward, both of soft burgundy leather that matched the rest of the interior. Between both seats was enough legroom for even Clem Pickett. In one corner was a television set. In the other corner, a telephone and fax machine.

Lisa and Ralphy ignored Mike as they flicked television stations—with a remote control, of course. Joel sat hunched over his teddy bear on the other end. In other words, things were nearly normal.

There was a slight click from Ralphy's corner, and I looked up to an explosion of white.

"Ralphy," I groaned as soon as my eyes cleared, "next time give a guy warning."

"No problem," he said, grinning. "As long as you promise to

keep those stupid expressions on your face. Why else would I take these candid shots?"

Can I help it—as Ralphy has proved with his camera again and again—if I get lost in thought and a dumb frown of concentration makes me look goofy?

"Thanks, pal," I said. "See if—"

I didn't get a chance to finish my threat. Amanda clicked open the driver's door.

"That's it, lady and gentlemen. We drive around, load your luggage into your rooms, and then find a restaurant. Anyone have a problem with that?"

It had been at least three hours since our in-flight meal. I sincerely hoped Amanda didn't expect anyone to answer yes.

"Ricky, there's a good reason I don't have a Florida accent," Amanda said after carefully chewing and swallowing a bite of steak. "Like most people in this state, I wasn't born here."

"Good thing." Mike spoke through the french fries about to enter his mouth. "If too many people were born in this restaurant, they'd never have time to serve food."

"Ignore him," Lisa told Amanda. "Starvation makes his brain weak."

"Exactly," Mike said. "Can we order more fries?"

I sighed. "Mike, maybe just once could we listen?"

Amanda, however, smiled—something she did often if the slight upward wrinkles around her eyes were any proof. Her short, straight brunette hair curved around her face and ended just below her jawline. She had a delicate nose, precisely straight teeth with just a slight gap between the two front ones, and pearl white skin. It made a good picture.

"Hey, guys," Amanda continued with her smile, "let me tell you. Nice light conversation is just fine after years of driving big-bellied businessmen who think the world should revolve around them just because they have money."

She caught my impatient glance. "And yes, Ricky, I'll finish explaining."

She set down her knife and fork. "I moved to Florida about two years ago. Before that I was employed by Jericho Stone's movie company in L.A. It was great to hear from him again when he called and asked if I could spend a few days showing you guys the sights until your parents arrived."

Mike tapped her elbow. "Mind if I finish your potato?"

"Not at all," Amanda said. "You mind if I ask how come Mr. Stone arranged this trip?"

"I'll explain," Lisa volunteered. "Mike'll be too busy eating, and Ricky has to track down his brother."

Aaaack. Joel is gone already?

I stood in half panic.

"I saw him headed to the coatroom," Lisa added.

I breathed thanks and dashed away as Lisa started to tell Amanda about the movie shooting adventure we'd experienced at a zoo near Hollywood. I found Joel shyly accepting a safety pin from the coat-check girl, and I hauled him back to the table. I took his teddy bear as security and held it on my lap below the table to save the embarrassment of being seen in public with it.

Lisa was just finishing the Jericho Stone explanation.

"Too cool," Amanda said. "And this is your first visit to Florida for all of you?"

We nodded, though I noticed that didn't slow Mike's food intake for a second.

"Then I'll tell you more," Amanda said. "First of all, that accent you asked me about. About a thousand people a day move into the state. You can see why there aren't too many people who can say they were born and raised here. Besides, if you're wondering about that big man, you mean a cracker accent."

"Cracker?"

"Stick with your potato, Mike," I advised.

"Crackers," Ralphy said. "They're sort of like the hillbillies of Florida.

They've been here for generations, and they make their living in the back-woods."

Amanda laughed in surprise. "Exactly."

"It's a bad habit of his," I explained. "Scientific facts and trivia."

"Trivia," Ralphy said with a straight face. "From Latin. *Tri via*. Three roads. In Roman times that's where notices were posted, where three roads met and a lot of traffic would see the notices."

Amanda laughed again.

I steered back to the subject. I could not shake the picture in my mind of a giant man, head bowed, led away in handcuffs. "So Clem Pickett's a cracker?"

"I only heard him speak briefly," Amanda said. "But by his accent, I'd say that's a good guess. And the police who escorted him out of the building were not Orlando cops. I saw their car out front as I pulled up. They were county cops, but I didn't pay attention to which county."

"Hmmm," I said.

Lisa read my thoughts. "Remember the only thing he said as they handcuffed him? Something about expecting it to happen."

I had not forgotten. "It ties in, then. Cops from out of town, here to get someone who lives in the backwoods. But why?"

Mike shrugged, gulped down his last mouthful, and shrugged again. "Could be hundreds of reasons. I mean, the guy was an ex-con. Who knows what he did to deserve jail?"

"But . . ." I let my voice trail away. I was here to worry about a Disney World vacation, not a stranger who was already long gone.

I only wish I could have worried about the Disney World vacation for a while longer. Because when we got back to our hotel room, the door was open and all of the contents of our luggage were strewn across the floor.

CHAPTER 5

Getting caught with polka-dotted boxer shorts by Lisa Higgins is not a dream way to start a vacation. Especially when three pairs of those shorts are spread across the carpet for the police and hotel manager to admire with equal amusement as they stand in the middle of your room, sunlight coming in through the still open door behind them.

Our hotel was one with a dozen or so buildings scattered among palm trees, walkways, swimming pools, and tennis courts. Each two-story building held twenty or so rooms facing out on each side, so that all rooms opened to the outdoors.

Next to our room, located on the second floor, was the one that Lisa shared with Joel. That room was untouched.

"One last time," the skinny cop said as he consulted his note pad. "Nothing was stolen."

"Nothing," I repeated. "We had our money and wallets with us. The only thing worth stealing was Ralphy's camera, and lucky for him, it must have fallen behind a pillow when they shook open his suitcase."

"Then, no damage done," the other cop said.

No damage? How could I walk around Disney World with Lisa Higgins knowing I wore polka-dotted boxer shorts? That's the trouble with the kind of presents that grandmothers usually give you. Not much fun.

"No damage," the hotel manager said firmly, as if he wanted

us convinced of the same thing.

"Okay, then, you guys can start cleaning up now," the skinny cop said. "There's not much else for us to do. Thanks for being smart enough not to touch anything until we arrived."

"No problem." Mike grinned. "We watch enough television to know police procedure."

Both cops groaned.

"Excuse me," I said quickly before they could turn those groans into departures. "What happens when out-of-town police visit Orlando?"

"I'll bite," the skinny one said, shrugging. "Go to Universal Studios like all the other tourists?"

"No, no," Amanda said. She had a firm grip on Joel's hand. "He means when they have official business."

Amanda explained the county cops we saw at the airport and the arrest that had taken place.

"What county?"

It was Amanda's turn to shrug. "It's not like I knew this guy would get arrested. I was too busy worrying about meeting these kids."

"Well," the other cop began. He had big feet and a belly to match. "Generally, as a courtesy, cops from one area inform the home boys of their presence. But if this was a quick pickup, they probably didn't bother."

"Still, what reason would they have to arrest him?" I persisted. I guess I wasn't ready to completely forget the way Clem Pickett had bowed his giant head and meekly accepted the handcuffs. "I mean, the guy was just coming out of prison. It's not like he'd had any time to break the law again."

The skinny cop just shook his head. "He could have been a suspect in an old crime. Besides, county sheriffs tend to run things their own way, especially if it's a one- or two-man department out in the sticks. Maybe they had a good reason. Maybe they didn't."

Big Belly matched the uncaring expression of his skinny partner. "What does it matter, anyway?"

I held my hands out with my palms up and gestured at the mess in our hotel room. "This, maybe?"

I knew it was a stupid remark as soon as I blurted it out. I was dimly associating this crime with an unrelated arrest hours earlier and miles away.

"You got some imagination, kid," Big Belly said. And not with a grin, either. "Rooms get busted into all the time."

"Not here," the hotel manager said. His face was still red from all his apologies.

"Fine, fine," Skinny Cop said. He pointed to the walkie-talkie on his belt, which had squawked static again and again. "We gotta get going."

He turned to me. "Look, kid. You got a right to be upset. It's not fun seeing your underclothes spread all over tarnation. But don't worry. Even if it was connected, how would that ex-con know where you were staying? Believe me, whoever busted in did it on impulse. They probably got scared away by a noise, or they would have done a couple other rooms at the same time."

The radio interrupted him again. This time he held it to his mouth and answered, "We're on our way."

They left us with our mess.

CHAPTER 6

Less than an hour after breakfast Tuesday morning I discovered one of the solutions for peace all across the earth. Assemble the generals of hostile armies at Disney World's Magic Kingdom.

Foreign culture from all sides flowed over us as we stood in line with Amanda to get our tickets at the entrance. Three friendly Japanese tourists with shiny smiles and friendly bows in all directions. A man and woman with heavy, deep German accents as they labored in English to decipher a brochure. Excited chatter from two small girls with tied-back hair who spoke in a language so quick it made their conversation sound like a bubbly piano concerto. A tall, graceful woman from India with big brown eyes and a dark beauty spot high on her cheek. Her husband, with a turban on his head, standing on his toes to whisper in her ear, and their baby in a stroller in front of them.

There was one thing different about this from a gathering of the United Nations that you sometimes see on television. Here, everybody was smiling.

And for good reason.

How could anyone bother to cling to favorite hatreds and troubles when ahead the sun bounced bright from the high towers of the fairy-tale castle of the Magic Kingdom? Hotel robberies, ex-cons under arrest, and the horror of mid-flight caterpillar sandwiches seemed far away.

When I told Mom about it later, she, too, smiled, but for another reason. *"Hey, bud,"* she told me as she messed my hair and made me squirm at her affection, *"now imagine the kingdom God promises and how much better that will be for everybody, especially since His kingdom lasts forever."*

I rolled my eyeballs because she was right, and then I told her at least in God's kingdom I wouldn't have to spend what felt like twenty-five minutes flying behind elephant ears just to keep Joel happy while all my friends clicked photos of me trying to hide every time we circled past. Because that's exactly what happened less than half an hour after taking the monorail from the ticket gates to the entrance of the Magic Kingdom.

I rode Dumbo the Flying Elephant.

Not the Jungle Cruise. Not the runaway mine train of Big Thunder Mountain Railroad. Not the roller coaster of Space Mountain. Not the Indy Speedway race cars.

But Dumbo the Flying Elephant.

"Hey, Ricky!" Mike yelled from the crowd as once again we sped by at less than half a mile per hour. "Getting scared yet?"

Ralphy stood behind him, waving like crazy and clicking photos.

"Funny, Mike," I muttered. "Very funny."

Joel, behind me, merely tightened the grip of his arms around my waist. I sighed.

From our vantage point I saw the high spires of Cinderella's Castle in one direction. And what seemed like hours later—when Dumbo finished half of his thrilling circle—I watched with envy all the people lined up at "It's a Small World," waiting to see exotic, faraway lands.

Best of all, a quarter turn later and just before reaching Mike and Lisa and Ralphy and their screams of encouragement, I saw the white top of Space Mountain, our next destination.

Dumbo finally began to slow from still to dead still.

"Not going to throw up, Joel? Or have a heart attack?"

He missed my sarcasm.

"Thank you, Ricky," he said almost formally. "I'm glad you're my brother."

Now how could I feel?

Amanda gave me no chance to think about it.

"Follow me, gang," she said with a flourish as Joel and I reached them. "Space Mountain was promised. Space Mountain shall be delivered."

She and Lisa made quite a pair. Both were wearing faded blue jeans, Amanda with a loose white blouse tucked in and Lisa with a bright, short-sleeved T-shirt.

Mike, as usual, wore a shirt so colorful that here in the nearly tropical weather I expected him to be attacked by hummingbirds looking for nectar. Ralphy, hair sticking in clumps because of the humidity, and Joel and I tagged behind. Ralphy, the ingrate, refused to carry Joel's teddy bear.

I tried to ignore the occasional swiveling of camcorder carriers who decided to record the sight of a poor guy my age tightly holding a teddy bear. Can I help it if it's Joel's only weakness?

When he's asleep, you can have a band playing in his room or wave a steaming hot dog smothered with mustard under his nose and he won't wake. Wriggle one paw of his teddy bear and he sits up instantly, staring at you with big accusing eyes. He won't go anywhere without it.

Since I could not imagine the terror of Joel lost among thousands of people on hundreds of acres of amusement park, I grimly bore the burden of his teddy bear.

"Nuts," Ralphy blurted.

"Drop another ice cream cone?" Lisa called back.

"Hah, hah," he said without lifting his head. "My camera is going strange on me."

He squinted at the back of it as we walked.

"Sorry, ma'am," he mumbled two seconds later after bouncing off a fat lady who held a kid with each hand.

Ralphy remained focused on his camera problem. "Yesterday I was on frame fifteen. This morning I've taken a dozen or more shots, and now I'm only on sixteen."

We kept walking, dodging grown-ups who took every step with those camcorders stuck to their faces. I guessed they'd rather enjoy their vacation back home in front of a television set than while they were actually in Florida.

"Hey, Ralphy," Mike commented, "maybe you forgot to load film."

"What am I? Stupid? Nobody would ..." Ralphy fiddled with a button on the camera. "Impossible!" He said nothing else.

Directly ahead loomed the high white dome of Space Mountain.

We took twenty more steps. And ten more sideways shuffles to avoid strollers or kids or photographers.

"Amanda," Ralphy began, "I need film."

We all stopped in a tight group.

"That's too bad, Ralphy," I said with as much sympathy as I could muster. "Does this mean no photographs of me and Dumbo? No photographs of me looking goofy in the limo?"

Ralphy shook his head. "And no photos of Mike in the hotel bathroom checking his nostrils for hair."

"What!" Mike yelped. "When did—"

Amanda interrupted. "We should stick together. It's too easy to get lost here. Why don't Mike and Ralphy go with me to get film?"

She pointed to a bench. "Lisa, Ricky, and Joel, you go ahead to Space Mountain and then meet us at this bench in thirty minutes. That should be long enough, since your Fastpass designated ride time is coming up. No point in all of us missing out on it."

We nodded, and I was grateful once again that we had such a cool chaperone, one who knew the ins and outs of avoiding the long lines at Disney World.

At Space Mountain we reached a sign with a horizontal line that warned that children under the height of that line could not go on the ride.

The top of Joel's head did not reach the line.

"I'll stay with Joel and we'll wait here for you," Lisa assured me. "Go ahead. I know this is the one ride you wanted the most."

I handed her Joel's teddy bear.

What a girl, I thought with admiration.

Until the roller coaster deep inside Space Mountain scared me green. It's one thing to drop like a rock tied to a falling piano. It's another thing not to see that drop coming. The Space Mountain roller coaster ride took place in pitch blackness.

I screamed myself hoarse each horrifying turn and shouted at the darkness for another chance at good old Dumbo.

Naturally, two minutes after the ride was finished and by the time I reached the exit of the walkway, I was hoping to try it just once more. Maybe Amanda would watch Joel and let the rest of us scare ourselves to death all at the same time.

I didn't get the chance to ask. As I blinked my way into the sunlight, two policemen in plain clothes were waiting for me.

CHAPTER 7

"Ricky Kidd."

Heavy southern drawl. It wasn't a question.

They both wore nylon baseball jackets, despite the sun, which was already hot at midmorning.

"Yes?" I said.

The first one smiled and reached into his jacket pocket. He flipped me his badge, a heavy silver star. "Sorry, son. Shoulda showed this right off the bat."

Right off the bat sounded like *rat offen the ba-et.*

"Police?"

He nodded. His reddish-brown hair was cropped short, and his shoulder muscles pushed hard against the fabric of his jacket. "It's about Clem Pickett."

"Sure. But what—"

"Just a few questions," his partner said. Same haircut. Same southern accent. It sounded like *jest ay fee-uhg kestshuns.*

"Okay." I looked across them. "Hey, Lisa! Over here."

Partner One snapped his head to look in the direction of my frantic waving.

"It's the girl," he said. "And the little kid."

Lisa and Joel hurried up to us.

"They're police," I explained. "Want to know about Clem Pickett."

Lisa's eyes narrowed. "Police? What about their uniforms?"

Partner Two chuckled, but it seemed to take him effort. "Well, ma'am, we didn't want to make the good folks round here nervous on their vacations. Seems people naturally associate police with trouble, and that sure ain't the case now."

Partner One nodded agreement. "Just a few questions."

Lisa stepped back and looked them over closely. "It seems strange that you would go to the effort of finding us in here."

Partner Two sighed.

"She does have a point, sir," I said as another thought struck me. "And how did you know who we were? Or how to find us here?"

Partner One closed his eyes briefly. His voice held less patience this time. "One, Clem Pickett told us your name. Your brother is Joel Kidd, right?"

I nodded.

"It took some time," Partner Two said, "but we traced you to your hotel. Police do have those connections. We got there just as you were leaving. We followed you in your big limo to the Magic Kingdom exit—we didn't feel it would be right to pull you over just for a few simple questions—and lost you in the traffic in the parking lot. It took us till now to find you."

"Satisfied?" Partner One asked Lisa. "It's not like we wanted to waste a morning like this, either."

Lisa nodded. "Sorry."

"Now," Partner One said, "tell us what Clem Pickett gave you just before he was arrested."

"Huh?" I blurted. Then I could picture Mom frowning at me for being rude. "I mean, pardon me?"

"Clem told our partners he gave you something. He's changed his mind and wants it back."

"Not me," I said.

Partner Two shrugged. "No problem, son. We figured he was sending us on a wild goose chase. We'd appreciate a statement, though. It'll really help us on this case."

He must have noticed my eyes grow wide with curiosity.

"Case?"

"We'll tell you about it on the way to our car. We've got all our paper work there."

Lisa broke in. "We have to wait for Amanda."

"We surely don't need all of you for this," Partner One said. "Our car is parked out front. Why don't y'awl go ahead and tell her that Ricky'll be back in twenty minutes."

Lisa shook her head. "We should wait. It's too easy for us to get separated and lost."

"It's not a big deal, Lisa. Just stay with us," I said quickly. "I'm sure Amanda and Mike and Ralphy won't mind waiting another few minutes at the bench for us."

Lisa pulled me aside and whispered in my ear, "This is too weird, Ricky. I don't like it."

I laughed in a short, low burst. "Maybe we'll learn more about Clem Pickett. Besides, what can go wrong? These guys are cops."

"Fine," she said. But her tightly pursed lips told me it wasn't. Still, she followed us to the monorail station.

Minutes later both cops escorted us to a plain brown sedan. Two antennae showed it held a police radio. The plastic bubble of a light flasher rested on the dashboard. I had no doubt it was a police car.

"See, Lisa?" I said. "Real cop car. Real cops. What's there to worry about?"

Partner One opened the back door.

"Git inside," he said.

"Inside? But I thought you—"

"Inside." He opened his jacket and patted his gun. "Before I shoot holes in your brother or your girlfriend."

CHAPTER 8

What could I do? Run?

Not when it meant leaving Joel or Lisa behind.

I pushed Joel ahead of me into the backseat. At least there he was farthest away from the man with the gun. Then Lisa in the middle, then me.

It was not the best time to complain at how the vinyl seats nearly blistered the back of my legs, even through my jeans, or that the air inside was stale and choking hot.

But I would be lying to say the growing puddles of sweat on my forehead were simply from the sun-baked interior. I was scared.

Partner One closed the backseat door on me and smiled an alligator grin downward. Partner Two walked around to the other side.

He pulled a sealed ziplock bag from his pocket. Through the clear plastic I could see a small white piece of cloth.

I didn't understand until he pulled the door open, snapped open the bag, pulled the cloth from the bag, and leaned down to Joel.

I gagged as a whiff of sharp sweetness slapped my nose.

He pressed the cloth against Joel's face. Within seconds Joel slumped against Lisa's shoulder.

"One down," Partner Two announced.

He reached across Joel.

Lisa punched him hard in the face. He blinked once but showed no other reaction.

She tried pulling his arm away, but he swatted her efforts aside.

She, too, slumped within seconds.

"Two," he said. Still no emotion in his voice.

He hunched across Joel and Lisa and stared in my face.

A tiny trickle of blood escaped the corner of his mouth. He licked it clean.

"Try anything," he said, "and I'll break your nose. That's a promise."

Sadness surprised me. I figured I had maybe five seconds left of the rest of my life, and what filled me was sadness. Not life flashing before my eyes, but an ache for what there was to leave behind. Mom, Dad, friends, the arc of a baseball against blue sky, the electricity of an unseen fish bumping the bait, the smell of leaves on a warm September day, that kind of stuff.

Partner Two pushed the cloth roughly against my face.

My eyes opened wide. Half because of the terrible sweetness that squeezed a drowning blackness into my temples. And half from more surprise because of another realization that faded as I dropped into that blackness.

I wasn't scared anymore.

CHAPTER  9

A Space Mountain roller coaster ride had nothing on the torture that bounced me awake some time later.

It was dark, as pitch black as it had been on the roller coaster. The twists and turns were just as unexpected. And I felt like screaming.

Except Joel's foot was in my mouth.

At least I hoped it was Joel's foot.

"Anybody awake?" I croaked.

The object embedded against my teeth stirred and pulled away.

"Joel?" My voice did not improve with continued use.

In the darkness there was a twisting and turning of a small body; a tiny hand brushed my leg and then found my hand. It squeezed tight.

"Joel!"

"I'm awake, too," Lisa's voice said. "But I'm not sure I want to be."

Another hard bounce flung me upward.

Ouch!

I landed on a flat circle. A tire?

Finally it made sense. My eyes began to adjust. Tiny cracks of light seeped into the edges of the darkness. Dust filtered downward to clog my eyes and mouth. That loud hum in the background translated into the sound of a motor—not my pounding headache as I had first suspected.

We were in the trunk of a car.

That answered, another part of my mind struggled with a question that made less sense. Yes, we had been kidnapped.

But why?

For a long time all I could think of was how badly I wanted the terrible ride to end.

We were folded and cramped. The trunk was suffocatingly hot. And because of the knockout drug—maybe chloroform?—I felt like throwing up with every breath of dust and air.

Then the ride stopped, and I realized exactly what that implied. Our kidnappers would be doing one of two things. Leaving us inside. Or taking us out.

Neither prospect filled me with great joy. I half wished we were still being rattled around like bags of potatoes.

One car door slammed. Then another.

Two people, maybe more. The same cops?

Slow footsteps. But no slapping of leather on pavement, no crunching of shoes on gravel.

A dirt road?

Then a pause that took forever.

Joel squeezed my left hand. With my other hand I squeezed Lisa's. During those terribly slow moments my mind ran wild. Maybe they were getting ready to push the car over a cliff. Maybe they were going to pour gasoline on the car and light a match.

The silence continued.

Or maybe they were just going to walk away and leave us trapped.

"Now, ah tole you a hunnerd times already," a voice reached into the trunk. "It ain't like real kidnapping. We jus' git what the boss ordered, bring 'em back up the road, and send 'em packing. No harm done."

A jangling of keys, then the scratch of metal against metal as a key clicked home in the lock. The lid popped open.

"Take care your mask don't slip." Those words were the only warning we had that identical twin rubber faces were waiting above us in the glare of white heat.

"Out."

We didn't need a second invitation. Not when our legs and arms had been pretzels for so long.

I felt unsteady on my feet. Lisa seemed to, too. She leaned against me for support.

"Halloween?" Joel giggled, clutching his teddy bear.

I wished I were young enough to believe this was some kind of game.

"Funny, kid." The mask muffled the man's voice, but even so, I could tell he was not one of the cops who had kidnapped us from Disney World.

My eyes blinked away the pain of sudden sunshine. I gaped at their appearance. The rubber faces—above checkered flannel shirts—had long and wobbly skinny noses, high bald foreheads, and chins that jutted out as far as the noses.

The taller of the two answered my unspoken question. "Kid, what yer staring at is lifesaving devices."

I squinted in continued puzzlement.

"Yep," the taller one continued. "You cain't see our faces. Thataway, after you help us out, we can set you free. 'Cause if you'd be able to identify us later, why, we'd have to leave you in the swamps as tasty tidbits for a big ol' alligator."

He didn't have to say any of it twice for me to understand either part. The identification. Or the swamp and the alligator.

We were on a narrow trail of tire tracks in red clay dirt, separated by tired brown grass. Large oak trees guarded the road, each draped with beards of grayish green Spanish moss that clung to the branches like torn fog.

Beneath those trees was a green wall of underbrush and ferns. And, more ominous, in all directions were scattered pools of black water that glinted occasional disks of sunshine.

As if to confirm our isolation, insects buzzed a frantic and uninterrupted whine. The humid heat pressed upon us, bringing with it the smell of oozing mud filled with half-decayed vegetation.

It made me think not only of alligators rising from the depths like primitive monsters but of cottonmouth snakes, black widow spiders, and bottomless bogs.

In other words, the man behind the mask would not have to threaten us for long with big ol' alligators to get whatever he wanted. I was immensely grateful not to have seen their faces, not to have them worried about whether we could identify them later.

"What help do you need?" Lisa asked. "And why bring us here for it?"

"Ma'am, I reckon on only answering the first question. And what we need is a simple contribution from your friend," the first mask replied as he nodded in my direction.

Me? What do I have to give that is worth a kidnapping?

We waited.

The masked man faced me squarely.

"Kindly return the coin that Clem Pickett left with y'awl."

CHAPTER 10

Coin?

Asking that would be the logical reply. I had no idea what coin they meant.

But a sudden thought stopped me. They had been desperate enough to have us kidnapped in bright sunshine from one of the biggest amusement parks in the world. How would they react to discover their insane crime had been for nothing? And how much chance was there that they would just shrug and apologize before letting us go?

Not much chance at all, I decided without needing to strain many brain cells.

So I didn't respond to his question by asking what coin. I tried to buy time and information without making either of them angry.

"Not to mean disrespect, sir, but don't you think it would be dumb to carry a coin that important in my back pocket?"

The shorter of the two masked men snorted. "Lookit, son. It weren't in your hotel room. Where else it gonna be but in your back pocket?"

The other masked man reached over and whacked his partner across the shoulder. "They ain't s'posed to know 'bout the hotel."

Number One whined but said nothing else.

Number Two turned his attention to me. "Son, jus' hand it

over. Y'awl got my word we'll drive y'awl back thataway and set you loose. You'll be back at your hotel in time for supper."

I took a deep breath. "I don't have it."

Not that I wanted to let him know I'd never had it, either.

Number Two shook his head. "Son, I'm truly sorry to hear you say that."

Number Two nodded at Number One.

Before I could blink, the shorter masked man had pounced on me with the strength of ten panthers. He forced me facedown into the red dirt and poked and prodded my clothes. Just before I'd breathed half of the county's soil, he flipped me on my back. He remained standing and kept his foot against my throat.

Joel fought Mask Number Two in efforts to reach me. I rolled my eyes and tried to shake my head no as he struggled.

"Empty them pockets," Mask Number Two ordered me. He didn't even grunt at the effort of holding Joel motionless.

I emptied them. My wallet. A Magic Kingdom ticket. Three quarters, a dime, and a Mickey Mouse key chain.

"That ain't real good news," Mask Number Two said. He held Joel in place with a tight grip on his shoulder. "Where'd you hide it, son?"

I tried to speak. My words came out as a gargle.

Lisa's face was pale. A spot of rose on each cheek betrayed her anger.

Mask Number Two made a head motion. Mask Number One took his foot off my throat, helped me to my feet, and dusted off my back with great thumps of his hand.

I coughed and fought tears of rage and frustration at being so helpless.

"Where'd you hide it?" Mask Number Two repeated.

We'd be left in the swamps as alligator food if he knew Clem Pickett had given me nothing but a handshake.

Stall, I told myself.

I wiped my face with the back of one hand, then with the back of the other.

"How do you know Clem Pickett doesn't have it?" I finally asked.

"That's a durn stupid question, son. The less'n you know, the less'n your chances of getting kilt."

Good point, *very good point*, I reminded myself. So much for good grades on stalling techniques.

My mind raced in tight, scrambled circles.

Then I knew what to try next.

"If you had a coin that important," I said, "wouldn't you take insurance precautions? Like mailing it someplace safe?"

"Thass right!" Mask Number One began. "I'd do exactly that. Why—"

A cutting motion from Mask Number Two silenced him. Number Two then scratched at his rubber forehead. "The boss ain't gonna like this. None at all."

Mask Number Two stared at me again. It chilled me, seeing only the whites of his eyes as proof there was a face behind that eerie rubber.

"Mailed it, huh? Where?"

I shrugged. "It would probably be smart to mail it back to Clem, wouldn't you say?"

Strange, not wanting to flat-out lie to a kidnapper, like maybe Mom would be proud of me, even though that should have been the least of my worries. But so far I'd only asked hypothetical questions. I hadn't said I had the coin or even actually told him I had mailed it.

Mask Number Two snapped his fingers, as if coming to a decision. Then he pointed directly behind us.

"Y'awl get back inside."

We hesitated.

He pushed Joel directly back at us.

"Now. Afore I git riled."

Lisa moved in first. I followed. Then Joel.

Just before Mask Number One shut the trunk, I held up my hand. "The teddy bear, sir. My brother dropped it on the ground. Could you...?"

Mask Number One clucked and bent to retrieve it.

Mask Number Two shook his head and directed his words at me. "Son, let me tell you something about Clem and that coin. It ain't worth it. Protecting the property of a man what murdered his only uncle."

Murder.

The trunk lid shut us back into darkness.

CHAPTER 11

How long could we stay curled in balls tiny enough to fit into a baking hot oven that pitched and bucked worse than a wild bronco?

The answer was simple. As long as it took for someone to stop the car and let us out. Because we had no other choice.

I almost wished that they had knocked us out again. Bruises began to form on bruises, and when we tried conversation, more pitching and bucking would knock us breathless. The ride would have been a lot more enjoyable unconscious.

"Understand, Lisa?" I repeated. Talking was difficult enough in the dust and heat and over the squeaks of car springs, but in explaining my evasiveness about Clem Pickett's coin, I also needed to be as quiet as possible. I didn't know if my voice would carry to the interior of the car.

"If they know we don't have it," I wheezed between bumps, "they might decide never to let us go."

"But how long can we—*ouch!*—stall them?" she managed, half before a huge pothole, half after.

"At least until a few days of mail arrives at Clem's place. By then someone will have found us."

Silence, except for the car springs and rattling muffler.

"Right?" I asked. "Someone will find us by then, don't you think?"

"Of course," she said without conviction.

How could I fool myself into believing we had hope if I couldn't even fool her?

We stopped speaking and tried saving our energy. I consoled myself by thinking that at least Joel might believe we had a chance of survival.

More bumping.

It got so bad that I decided I'd much rather try sleeping in a cement mixer. Or if not a cement mixer, then a—

Hey!

Another thought struck me.

To confirm that thought, I tried picturing Clem Pickett's last few moments before arrest.

Clem had squatted to his knees and looked Joel square in the face to say good-bye. Still on his knees, he had reached out to shake Joel's hand. And then he'd stood and turned to shake my hand.

That's what the cops—if they were real cops—had seen as they ran up to the luggage carousel in the airport. Clem and me. Not Clem and Joel.

But it was with Joel that Clem had become friends.

What if . . .

"Joel!" I whispered into the darkness. "Remember the big man on the airplane? The one who ate your caterpillar?"

"He said sorry about eating it," Joel reminded me. "He was nice."

"Great." I waited for a lull between bumps. Clem Pickett was fresh out of prison for murdering his only uncle, but he apologizes for chomping a caterpillar to death. "Glad to hear it, pal. But did he give you anything? Like a coin?"

"No coin. But where he lives."

"Huh?—OUCH—What was that?" I was getting really tired of the tire jack and the way it was slowly deforming my ribs.

Joel spoke louder. "Where he lives. For being a . . ." His hesitation was clear, even in the darkness. ". . . a . . . a . . . pen. . . ?"

"Pen pal!" Lisa finished for him. "They must have traded addresses."

I groaned.

Only Joel was capable of making friends with the one person on an airplane who could lead us into a disaster like this. The worst part was not knowing much else about how bad the disaster was. Like, who were those cops? How had they managed to identify Joel and me among the crowds of people in Disney World? How had the kidnappers known which hotel room—out of the thousands in Orlando—belonged to us? And what was so important about a single coin?

Another bump slammed my head into the top of the trunk.

The only thing I knew was why Clem Pickett had been thrown in jail. Murder.

I hoped our kidnappers didn't approve of *his* type of crime.

Blindfolds were hardly necessary—by the time the car stopped and they hauled us out of the trunk, we were so dazed we wouldn't have known an alligator from a frog.

But Mask Number One and Mask Number Two blindfolded us anyway as soon as they pulled us from the trunk. Not, however, before I saw our next method of transportation.

An airboat. One of those wide, lightweight aluminum boats with a giant fan at the back end. I'd seen one in a movie, and Ralphy—naturally Ralphy—had explained.

Airboats are made for traveling across extremely shallow water or through reeds—shallowness or reeds that would foul a boat motor in seconds. The boat itself barely needs any depth to stay floating, and the giant fan blows air backward, just like an airplane's propeller.

It did little for my hopes to get that glance at the airboat docked to a buckling wooden pier. Airboats are designed to do one thing: take people away from civilization.

We weren't going to be back at the hotel in time for supper.

CHAPTER 12

"It ain't no castle, but y'awl kin call it home," Mask Number One drawled as he removed our blindfolds.

I swayed slightly to keep my balance. Hours of swishing back and forth in a light boat traveling at high speeds will do that to you for your first five minutes on land.

"Just leave the blindfold on," I muttered.

"What's that you say?" Mask Number One asked.

"Nothing, sir."

Being blindfolded had been a mercy. We stood beside a single tree near the shore, facing our new home. One quick look in the late afternoon sun told me that this shack was the last place I wanted to call home.

Beneath the shade of other, smaller trees, the shack leaned in five different directions. Vertical gray white planks for walls. Rough holes sawed in vague squares for glassless windows. A door clinging half open on one hinge. A battered sheet tin roof.

Mask Number Two caught my less than approving stare of appraisal.

"It ain't the Ritz, but it oughter keep the panthers out."

"Wonderful, sir."

Joel left us and wandered to the shack. He held his teddy bear in his left hand. He peeked past the door, then looked back at me and grinned. He disappeared inside.

"Little feller takes to it like a bear to honey, don't he?" Mask

Number One said.

Mask Number Two grunted. "He'd better. They ain't escaping."

Something about Joel's grin bothered me. I'd seen that special one before but couldn't remember when.

Mask Number One poked me in the ribs. "Got that? Y'cain't escape."

That, I could plainly see.

From where we stood at the side of the airboat, there were maybe twenty steps to the front of the shack. Beyond it—almost the same distance—the water started again. On both sides, the same. Water and trees perched on gnarled roots. But no land connecting us to the opposite shore.

Wonderful. A shack on a small low island in the middle of green black water at least two hours by airboat from the nearest road and held hostage for a coin I'd never seen. So much for my dream vacation.

A slight banging of wood against wood reached us from the interior of the shack.

"See what that durn boy is doing," Mask Number Two ordered.

Mask Number One shrugged and began the twenty steps across the soft ground.

It came back to me. Joel's grin. I'd seen it once before, the day he—

"I cain't see him!" Mask Number One called back from the open doorway. "No, there he is. Under the table."

The man stepped inside. "Come out from under that, you little rascal," we heard.

Silence.

It was a grin that said Joel had—

"I said, git out from under that," his voice reached us. "Do I gotta drag y'out by your shoes?"

"Sir?" I began to Mask Number Two. "Maybe—"

Too late.

We heard a loud clunk. As if Mask Number One had stood straight up in panic without remembering he was bent underneath a table to grab Joel's shoes.

Rapid scuffling.

Silence.

Then an excited voice barely muffled by the rubber mask.

"Leave him be, son. That . . . that ain't no kitty."

I closed my eyes and winced because I'd been right. That *had* been the grin that said Joel had found a wild animal, the grin to match exactly the one he'd beamed the morning he'd spotted two baby raccoons underneath our porch.

"Come on, son. Please. Point him the other direction. He's getting nervous, son. Don't—!"

Mask Number One interrupted his own voice with an enthusiastic roar of mingled rage and fear that didn't diminish by one decibel during his entire sprint from the front door of the shack to his headlong dive into the water behind us.

We understood within seconds. The force of the smell was like getting hit in the face with a wet cat.

Just as quickly, Mask Number One leaped out of the water again. "What was I thinking?" he shouted. "That could kill me, too!"

I didn't have time to wonder long at what he meant.

Joel staggered out, glassy-eyed and as dazed as I've ever seen him.

And on Joel's heels, an equally dazed skunk. It looked left, then right, then limped for cover beneath the nearest bushes.

CHAPTER 13

The ringing of a telephone woke me.

Telephone? But aren't we stuck in the swamps? Maybe I'd been dreaming and if I simply opened my eyes I'd see the hotel phone and discover . . .

"Yeah, they're here," Mask Number Two's voice sounded. "But we got some problems."

Silence in the darkness—except for the buzzing of mosquitoes that swarmed my head. More awake now, I knew I wouldn't have to open my eyes to discover I was still lost in the swamps. It must now have been a couple of hours after sunset. I could feel the rough fabric of a blanket around me, the smear of insect repellant all over my face, and I saw the pinpoints of stars above. My back hurt from leaning against the cold rough bark of a tree. Worst of all, there was the skunk smell of Joel, downwind in his blanket.

"Yeah, problems. Nothing tomater juice cain't fix."

Silence again.

Lisa stirred in her blanket beside me. She, too, was now awake.

"Tomater juice," Mask Number Two repeated with impatience. "Fer a dad-blamed skunk. And I ain't in no mood to discuss it."

A groan reached us from the airboat—now anchored offshore—where Mask Number One was huddled in isolated misery. He had taken most of the skunk spray. I couldn't imagine how bad that might be. Joel had only been hit with some of the drifting mist, and he still smelled like the fog of fried onions hidden in smelly socks, except a thousand times worse.

"Yeah. Gotcha," Mask Number Two said. He had a flashlight in one hand, the phone tucked against his shoulder, and it looked like he was taking notes with his other hand. "Uh-huh. Gotcha. Yeah. A couple days, then. Yeah, I'm looking forward to gettin' outter here, too."

Click.

The man stood from his perch on a folding chair halfway between us and the boat. He set down the flashlight and fumbled with something atop the pile of equipment beside him that they had loaded off the boat shortly before sunset.

There was a scratch and a flaring of a match. Within moments a gas lantern hissed and sputtered light across our small island.

"Hey, wake up!" he called in our direction. "Except for the short 'un. He kin stay behind in that blanket."

I stretched myself to alertness as I rose to my feet. I had long earlier decided there was no chance of trying to fight. Mask Number Two did not seem a gentle man, and I needed an extra hundred pounds before considering a wrestling match with him. And even if I was lucky enough to overpower him, where could we go from this island?

He motioned us over to him. The long shadows of his arm reached across from the lantern like an eerie ghost.

"Yer friends are awaiting," he told us as we walked over. "Awaiting fer a call announcing y'made it home safe 'n' sound."

He must have seen the confusion on my face.

"Son," he said, "we want that coin bad. Bad 'nough to have them police at Disney World go back in and tell your chauffeur that you and the girl and the boy had to rush to catch a flight home to tend to your maw, who had an unexpected seizure."

He twisted his arm to look at his watch. "It's nine o'clock. You call the hotel and tell 'em your maw's ailing a bit but the worst is over. Otherwise Big Ben ..."

I must have still looked confused.

"It's a cellular phone, boy. We're from the sticks, but that don't mean we're ignorant of cellular phones and technology."

I knew it was a cell phone. It was the mention of someone named Big Ben that had me confused.

I nodded, not knowing what else to say.

He handed me a piece of paper, then dialed the phone.

"You speak to that chauffeur lady. You say exactly what's on this'n here paper. Anything else, and your brother'll be alligator food—that is, iffen Big Ben can stomach something what smells as bad as him."

Who is Big Ben? But I didn't have time to ask.

He shoved the phone at me and it was already ringing.

I could hardly read the words beneath the lantern light. I pulled the paper closer just as Amanda answered.

"Hello?" Cool and unconcerned.

"Hello?" I said. I wanted to scream for help.

"Ricky!" Pleasure and a trace of worry. "Your mother's fine?"

"Yes," I answered, reading the script in front of me. "They thought it might be a stroke, but it turned out to be a serious allergy attack. We should be back as soon as another flight is available."

"That's good," Amanda replied. "We didn't know what to think when those policemen explained. But then we thought it was a miracle that their partners found you so quickly and managed to get you to the airport in time for that flight. It must have been fun—sirens and all—as they rushed you there."

My heart dropped lower and lower. Nothing in her voice indicated concern.

"Great fun," I said.

Mask Number Two made cutting motions across his throat, then pointed in the direction of the water.

"Well, I should go," I said, reading from the script again. "I'll be calling in a couple of nights. Hope you and the guys enjoy the Epcot Center."

"Okay, Ricky," she said cheerfully. "We're just glad to hear it was nothing serious. Talk to you later."

"Bye now," I said as she hung up.

Mask Number Two reached for the phone.

"Done good, kid. Big Ben'll have to wait awhile for your brother."

"Big Ben?" Lisa made the mistake of asking the question that was in my mind.

"Yup. Big Ben." Mask Number Two made an elaborate gesture of looking at his watch again. "Guess he's ready to put on a show."

He moved a cooler away from his pile of equipment and pried the lid open.

I was relieved to see it was full of food. That meant at least they intended to keep us alive for a while.

The man reached inside and pulled out a hunk of raw meat.

"Look at the situation this way," he said as he closed the cooler. "Your friends figure you're home, safe with your maw and paw. But no, you're on an island in a small bay in the middle of nowhere, and when we leave you here alone on the island tomorrow, there ain't no way for you to git back, even if you did know where to go. Even if you found a way off this island."

He laughed. "So we ain't in no rush for the coin to arrive at Clem's. And iffen it turns out you been lyin' and it don't arrive, we got Big Ben to help refresh your memory."

I had a growing feeling I didn't want to meet Big Ben.

Mask Number Two walked to the water. He carried the lantern with him and left us in a pool of darkness. From where Lisa and I stood, we saw everything much too clearly.

First, the man set the chunk of beef down on the land—one good stride away from the water. Then he squatted near the water and slapped the surface with his open palm. Six times he did that, loud smacks that echoed through the black air.

Then he stepped back several strides, still holding the lantern high.

Nothing happened for a few minutes.

Then there was a surge of water in the white light.

The surge grew. And grew.

And unbelievably, the blackness of that surging water became the glistening blackness of an alligator's snout. Then its broad head.

It pushed itself forward on those bent, short legs. Slowly.

Water streamed down from the top of its jaw, misting slightly in the cool night air. The alligator lurched ahead and grunted. Even four feet onto land—close enough to glare at the hunk of raw meat—not much more than its monstrous head and shoulders were out of the water.

Now I understood why Mask One had jumped out of the water so quickly after diving in from the skunk. I shuddered to think at how much of the beast still remained underwater. How easily it could clamp a human in its jaws.

Lisa clutched my arm at the same time I clutched hers. We did not step back, however. There was not a chance we wanted to attract the slightest bit of attention from those tiny, gleaming, evil eyes.

Another grunt and then a sudden slash of teeth that was only a blur of movement, and the meat disappeared.

The alligator raised its head a little higher, then grunted one last time before it slithered backward to disappear in the blackness.

I did not plan on sleeping ever again.

CHAPTER 14

I spent most of the night after that alligator show staring at the shadows cast in the moonlight by the battered shack and thinking how great those walls would've been for shelter without the gagging fumes of skunk spray, which still overwhelmed us from our resting spot twenty feet away in the open air.

That in itself was a good lesson on how much we have every day and how much we take for granted. The thought of spending time in that creepy old shack had seemed like punishment, until the alternative had become leaning against a Spanish oak with mosquitoes waiting for your insect repellent to wear thin while somewhere out in the water that lapped against shore an alligator the size of a dinosaur silently haunted the depths.

What I would have given for a dumpy bed and dry crackers. Or to be in the middle of the toughest math exam in the history of school. Or to be weeding thistles in Mom's garden.

Anything but where we were.

Every new night noise—and there were dozens—brought me forward, squinting into the dark. The slightest variation in the lapping of waves brought me to my feet, ready to flee Big Ben. And all that filled my mind—besides the longing for the inside of that shack—was one simple fact.

I did not have any knowledge of the coin they so desperately wanted.

Sleep did not arrive. So when the first rays of a false dawn surprised me into hope, my mouth was still dry with fear. And when Wednesday's real dawn did arrive a half hour later—pale gray slowly becoming blue—it was not hard to close my eyes and sink into the gratitude of prayer for still being alive.

Which only left us as many more dawns as it would take for our kidnappers to decide the coin would not arrive in Clem Pickett's mailbox.

"You oughter know that gators don't chew people to death. No sirree. Not even ones 'a size of ol' Big Ben."

Lisa grimaced politely beside me at those words and set the remainder of her bacon and eggs aside.

Mask Number Two continued. "Instead, what gators do is drown peoples. Takes 'em in their jaws, pulls 'em back into the water, and rolls over and over like a big wrestling match until they's drowned. After that, the gator hauls the body to some log underneath the water and pins it there fer a few days, till it's ripe and all softened up and ready fer good eatin'."

I smiled less politely and set my own food aside.

Joel walked over from his spot beneath a tree and took the plate. Easy for him to stay hungry—he was used to his own smell.

"Hey!" Mask Number One shouted from the boat. "Y'got breakfast for me out here? I could eat a raw snake!"

Mask Number Two picked up a few eggs from the carton and threw them at the boat. "Don't expect better service for lunch!" He then muttered at a barely heard level, "And I gotta spend the ride back in with that durn fool."

He caught our stares.

"Thass right. The two of us'll be leaving shortly. Which is why I want you to understand gators. You'd be fools to try 'n' escape. As you can plainly see, Moonshiner's Bay ain't that much more'n a overgrown pond. Big Ben knows everything that goes on in it."

Mask Number Two pointed at one of the shores on the other side of the water. "And even if you made it across, what dry land you'd get ain't gonna be much more'n brambles and cottonmouth snakes and pygmy rattlers. And you'd have dozens more swamps with dozens more gators after that."

As if we hadn't received that message last night. Very loudly. Very clearly. All it had taken was an alligator the size of your average truck.

He pressed on anyway. "And furthermore to all that, it's pert' near fifty miles to the nearest road. Three, maybe four hours by airboat."

He kicked dirt onto the fire that he had used to cook us breakfast.

"We're leaving you plenty a' food. None what needs cooking, though. 'Cause you cain't be getting any bright idears 'bout attracting help at nights with no fire."

Mask Number Two looked toward the airboat and sighed.

"Haul in the anchor!" he suddenly ordered across the water. "Bring the boat in and make me plenty a' room in the front. 'Cause you're doing the driving, and I aim to be upwind a' your stink the entire way."

CHAPTER 15

It took Joel less than half an hour to make me forget about our predicament. He wandered out from behind the shack with a copper-colored snake wrapped around his arm.

"These are our options, Lisa," I was saying at the time. "We can—aaaacckk!"

I dove past her shoulder, found a stick, rolled to my feet, and charged upon Joel.

Don't think, I told myself. *Just do something without giving yourself time to get scared.*

Somehow I'd have to distract the snake long enough to—

I skidded to a stop.

And sighed.

"Joel Kidd," I said. "One day. That's all I want. One day without you driving me crazy."

He smiled.

"Give me that," I said.

He stepped forward.

I held up my hand as a waft of skunk pounded my nose.

"Close enough, pal. Take it off your arm and throw it here."

He did.

I saw why I had been so easily fooled. It was copper tubing, spiraled in a long, lazy coil that he had wrapped around his arm. Why it would be on this isolated island made no sense to me.

I shrugged and turned back to Lisa.

"Silly kid," I told her. "Give him a junkyard and he'd be happy forever."

I tossed the tube aside and rejoined her.

"Options, you were saying?" she asked with her usual knowing smile. "I'm expecting a long and complicated theory which will do justice to your hardworking imagination."

I sighed again.

She placed a hand on my arm. "Just teasing. You usually come up with something that makes sense."

I brightened.

"Although," she quickly added, "it takes you forever to get there."

She laughed at the new expression on my face. "Let me sum it up for you," she said. "You and I don't have any idea which coin they want. Worse, we don't know why they want it. And while it might have been smart to buy time by suggesting you mailed it back to Clem, now it looks like we're in even more trouble. Because we're stuck here until they return."

"Yes, and—"

"And next—you'll want to announce grandly—they'll be gone until tomorrow night, which gives us two days to think our way out of our predicament."

"How did—"

"How did I know? Easy." She thumbed a finger to make each point. "One, when you spoke to Amanda last night, you were forced to say you'd call her in a few days, which means they *will* be back to make you call again. But two, they left at least two days' worth of food in the cooler, which means they don't expect to be back sooner. And three, he spoke to us about not making a signal fire, which means they aren't planning to be around tonight to watch us."

I sighed. My third in as many minutes.

She grinned. "You're not the only one around here who spends time thinking."

Worse for my male pride, I had to admit a tiny ray of hope. I betrayed it by asking, "Does this mean you have an idea to save us?"

It was her turn to sigh. "Not one."

We both stared at the water and said nothing.

Mask Number Two had been right. Moonshiner's Bay wasn't much more than an overgrown pond. A couple hundred yards in each direction, the tangled growth of trees and brush marked the opposite shorelines. At the far end lay the reed-filled channel the airboat had used for an exit.

I wanted a good reason to attempt crossing the water, though. We had seen enough of Big Ben the night before to keep me awake all of tonight, too.

Skunk smell hit us as Joel interrupted our somber mood.

"Crockpot," he announced.

"Right," I said. Then looked.

Joel held a clay jug, fresh dirt still clinging to its side. An earth-stained cork still plugged the narrow neck.

"Moonshiner's Bay," I blurted a half joke. "It'll be full of moonshine."

"Huh?" Lisa said.

"Moonshine," I said. "That's slang for home-brewed whiskey. You read about it in all the old detective mysteries."

She rolled her eyeballs skyward. "Sure thing. And that jug's full of booze."

"Pull the cork. It's not like you have anything better to do."

It took her five minutes of hard grunting before the cork released with a deep and hollow pop. Joel lost interest and wandered away while she struggled with it, which made breathing much more pleasurable.

Lisa sniffed the top of the jug. And gagged.

"This has got to be five thousand proof."

"Moonshiner's Bay," I repeated smugly, happy to finally contribute something in the way of deductions.

A second later I snapped my fingers. "Copper coils. Of course!"

"I don't understand," Lisa said.

"They were called stills," I told her. "During Prohibition people used stills to make whiskey."

She recorked the jug. "Prohibition. Didn't we just have a social studies class about that? It was in the 1920s or something."

I thought back to some of the mysteries I'd read. "Yup. Alcohol was outlawed across the country, so people began brewing it themselves and selling it illegally. That led to a lot of gang wars and stuff."

I thought out loud. "How were they set up again?"

"Gangs?"

I stood and paced. "No. Stills. I'm not quite sure exactly what they were, but if I remember correctly, they used fires beneath copper vats, which had tubes like—"

I grinned at a new thought. "Like reruns of that old television show. *M.A.S.H.* The doctors always had a little still in their tent with tubes of copper that dripped stuff into a jug. That, of course, explains the copper Joel just found."

I bowed low and made an elaborate sweep with my arms.

"Welcome, my dear," I said in my best theatrical voice, "to Moonshine Island."

"Enchanté," she replied.

"That's French, you bonehead," she added as I shot her a puzzled look.

"I knew that," I said quickly.

Silence between us again, and the happy mood that we had created soon leaked away.

My mind turned back to the still. In a few minutes I'd go to the effort of tracking Joel down—by using my nose, of course—and digging through what remained of the equipment.

Something, however, about the presence of a still on this small island bothered me. I thought longer about it, then about the shack.

The smallest of conclusions swirled dimly in the back of my head.

I told myself no. Especially because I didn't want to believe what it meant I should do next. Especially because of Big Ben.

And that led me to another thought. Why had Big Ben been so quick to answer those six slaps on the water?

The conclusion grew bigger and more concrete out of that swirl of thoughts.

Again I tried telling myself no.

But it didn't work.

"Lisa," I said in a voice of dread. "Somehow, I've got to get to the other shore."

CHAPTER 16

Lisa stepped closer to me and placed her palm against my forehead.

"This isn't good," she said. "Fifty miles from civilization, and you're delirious with fever."

"That's the whole point," I argued. "We're *not* fifty miles from civilization."

"But the guy in the mask said that we—"

I shook my head. "Put yourself in their shoes. You suddenly discover that the coin means a two- or three-day wait, depending on the mail system. And that means looking after three prisoners for all that time. Unless—" I swept my arms around us to indicate the leaning shack and the wilderness—"unless you find another prison guard."

Lisa shrugged. "I kinda figure all this swamp and the alligators make a great prison."

"Exactly," I said as I walked toward the shack. "And if we believe it is our prison, it will be."

Lisa followed.

"Okay, why *shouldn't* we believe them?" she asked. I could tell by her voice that she didn't understand my careful examination of the outside of the shack.

"Blindfolds, shacks, and stills," I answered almost absently.

I did not stop my examination of the loose boards. The skunk smell was rich enough to make me wince, even ten feet away from the shack.

"Do you find it hot?" Lisa asked.

That stumped me enough to get me to look at her instead of the shack. "Huh? Hot?"

"Like steaming hot? Hot enough to fry someone's brain?"

I stopped my pacing.

"Sorry, Lisa. I'll try to explain." I remembered what she had said about my convoluted imagination. "Without taking forever."

She smiled briefly and nodded.

"I couldn't figure why they'd go to the trouble of blindfolds. I mean, we'd seen them already, and they were wearing masks anyway. And with all those twists and turns, it's not like we would be able to memorize our way back if the trip really took three hours."

Lisa nodded again.

"So maybe they were trying to fool us into thinking the boat ride was that long," I said. "Maybe we were blindfolded so we wouldn't notice that, for example, they kept going in the same circles to make the ride seem longer than it is."

Lisa suddenly shook her head no. "And what if it really was a three-hour trip and there were things along the way they didn't want us to see?"

I moved away from the shack, picked up the copper tubing from where I had thrown it on the ground, and brought it back to her.

"This is from a still," I said. "Ask yourself why anyone would bother setting up a still fifty miles away from the nearest road. If that isn't enough of a hint, ask yourself why anyone would bother building a shack so far away."

"But—"

I shook my head. "No *buts*. I think those masked guys wanted to bluff us into staying. Who knows? A road might be less than a couple of miles from here."

Lisa frowned at me with enough intensity to stop a charging rhino. "Are you willing to bet our lives you're right?"

"Against the certainty that in two days we'll have to tell them we know nothing about their coin?" I rubbed my face with both hands at the decision I knew I'd already made. When I looked up, I said as simply as I could, "Besides, only one person's going to risk Big Ben."

Try being logical with a girl and nothing goes right. Shouting didn't help prove my point, either.

To me, there was no other choice.

No one was looking for us. Which meant not to expect any lost white knights or misplaced cavalries for miraculous rescues.

We had one night and two days to find a way out of our predicament, and there was no sense in risking all three of us.

Finally, if I was right, if there was a road close by, I'd be able to bring back help in plenty of time.

Lisa refused to see it completely my way. She agreed with me, all right, that someone had to make a break. The entire argument was not why but who.

Her anger burned the entire time I stripped pieces of wood from the shack.

"Have you heard of equality?" she fumed. "What gives *you* the right to play the hero and leave us here?"

The worst part was, I had no answer.

"Because I'd go crazy thinking about you trying to make it while I just waited helplessly?" I tried.

"Dumb male," she said. "And *I* won't go crazy with helplessness while *you're* out there?"

That's what I meant about her using logic. It was enough to drive me crazy. Especially because I couldn't come up with an answer for that, either.

"Why does this have to be a boy-girl thing?" I pleaded.

"Because once in a while you get on your high horse and forget we can do anything you can." She softened her words with a grin. "Never thought you'd be liberated in the middle of a swamp, did you?"

I held up my hands in front of me as if helplessly fending off an attack.

"Okay," I said. "You win. I shouldn't just assume things."

Then I grinned in return at a new thought. "But there is one reason I should go."

She stood hands on her hips, still half angry despite my best grin and the tongue I stuck out at her.

"What's that one reason?" she asked, picking up a clump of dirt.

"I thought of it first."

I ducked and laughed at how her throw missed my head.

The second clump caught me as I was straightening and left me with grit on my teeth for the next hour as we struggled to build a raft.

CHAPTER 17

I can't explain why I was so determined to be the one—instead of Lisa—looking for a nearby road.

Maybe it's that same urge you have when someone is cold and you lend them your sweater because it's more comfortable to be shivering yourself than to be warm and have to watch someone else shiver.

Or maybe it was stupidity caused by being a guy.

Whatever it was, I regretted it within three seconds of pushing off from the shore.

"Is the raft holding?" Lisa asked.

"Shhhhhhh!" I said with a frantic pointing at the water ahead of me. "He might hear!"

"Is the raft holding?" Lisa whispered.

"Yes," I croaked back.

"What?"

I tried again. This time I worked my jaws and tongue so that my mouth wasn't as dry as sand from the fear that was pounding my heart hard enough to send tidal waves.

"It's holding," I said. I tried not to look down at the five boards we had ripped from the wall of the shack and rigged as a bridge between two small oil drums, each sideways in the water. We had punched holes close together in the top half of each drum, using a log for a hammer and spikes for drill punches. Then we had run shoelaces and odd bits of rope through the holes and tied them around the planks. The raft would not take abuse, and even as I pushed away from shore with another plank that I used as a pole, the boards shifted back and forth too easily.

The drums—we had dug them from the heap of junk at the site of the still behind the shack—rode low in the water. Only the top three inches of each drum stayed above the water. That meant only three inches before the water poured into the punched-out holes beneath the boards. I was sure Big Ben's teeth were longer than that small gap of safety.

Lisa bit her lip anxiously as she waved good-bye.

In the movies she would have had a great exit line and mine would have been just as good and very noble.

But this wasn't a movie. I was kneeling on a raft that had a life expectancy shorter than a mosquito's, and riding it across green black water that might explode any second into a frenzy of thrashing monster whose only desire was to wrap his jaws around my stomach to drown me and haul my body to some underwater storage place.

I did not feel witty or noble.

I simply nodded good-bye to Lisa and Joel and concentrated on slow, careful pushes with the board. Neither Lisa nor I had to say anything; we both knew the terrible risk, even if Joel didn't. Because even if I made it to the far shore, there was still the terror of a cross-country search for a road that might or might not exist and that, if it did exist, might or might not lead somewhere safe.

There was the time pressure, too. It was already ten o'clock Wednesday morning. I had less than a day and a half to find some rescuers and return—if I could find my way back.

I shut that thought out of my mind, lifted the board slowly from the mud, and planted it farther ahead, ready to push again.

Every fiber and every nerve were totally focused on that simple movement. I could not afford to worry. It would be like getting five stories high on a ladder, then looking down and freezing with terror at your position.

Push. Lift. Plant. Push.

Push. Lift. Plant. Push.

Each new push put me into deeper water. More and more of the board disappeared into the murk each time.

A minute later the water was at least ten feet deep. I knew that because when I planted the pole, my hands dipped into the water.

That touch of wet was like a shock of electricity to remind me of the monster somewhere below.

I turned the board sideways and slowly, very slowly, used it as a paddle. Every minute only moved me a couple of yards closer to the far shore. But I knew if I paddled too quickly, my splashing might attract attention from the visitor of my nightmares.

The raft creaked to remind me that any speed would rip it apart.

I gritted my teeth and forced myself to continue that agonizingly slow movement of board against water. I realized what a rabbit must feel like when it lies low against the grass, not daring to break for safety as it trembles in hopes of not being seen.

Paddle. Push. Lift. Paddle.

Paddle. Push. Lift. Paddle.

Some deep instinct must have kept me from making noise, because I didn't know I had started crying until a fish jumped and the slight smack of its body falling back against water startled me into a half sob. Only then did I feel the tears that dropped onto the thighs of my jeans from my cheeks and top lip.

I knew then that I was that rabbit, ready to bolt from the grass into the jaws of a wolf simply to end the agony of suspense.

It was too tempting, the urge to scream and throw myself into the water. Anything but waiting pulse by pulse for Big Ben to raise his jaws in a surge of evil.

Then a new feeling touched me.

It was the same feeling that had surprised me in the backseat of the car when that one cop had covered my mouth and nose with a chloroform-soaked cloth, sending me into the black with no time to scream for the light to return.

The feeling was a certainty of faith much deeper than the one that I sometimes nod and smile and pray and sing along with in the safety of church without thinking about what it means. It was a feeling that I knew without question that God was there, always. It was a sudden sure feeling that the greatest fear on earth—of dying—had been conquered because of

Him and what He promised. The feeling that death was not a black and terrifying emptiness with no hope for me or the ones I might leave behind, that leaving earth might be sad and still frightening and something I should still fight against as hard as possible, but if it was to come, I could accept it with a calmness through His strength.

I can't lie. The tears still fell, and I was still scared. But behind the tears was a peace of knowing He would be there to receive me—now or later.

I paddled, probably grinning like a fool beneath those tears streaming down my face. And I paddled more.

Then my paddle hit ground. I poled the last twenty yards through shallow water, without bumping into an alligator.

CHAPTER 18

Nothing but the silence of sand and scrub pines greeted me.

It had taken at least five minutes to work through the thick underbrush and rotted logs that fringed Moonshiner's Bay. My shoes were already filled with oily mud, my jeans already torn above the right knee, and my face already scratched enough to bleed.

Still, I considered the dry sand and scrub pines to be good news. That meant higher ground. Away from alligators.

The bad news was how quickly I had lost a sense of direction. I knew, of course, that Moonshiner's Bay was behind me. But where was *behind*?

I had twisted and turned to avoid the worst of clawing vines. I had jumped and ducked fallen trees. I had splashed through shallow water. To keep a straight line would have been impossible, even with a compass. Without a compass I might as well have been blindfolded. Even looking back, I could not guess which bramble bush had been the final barrier to the small clearing guarded by the scrub pines where I now stood.

And time ticked by, second by second, minute by minute.

I paused long enough for my sweat to form lumps as big as the mosquitoes that formed a swarm above my head.

Another deep breath, and I pushed ahead.

Twenty more minutes of walking. Among the scrub pine trees progress was faster, though I hoped I wouldn't find my own tracks as evidence I was going in circles.

Humidity and heat punished me in small, steady punches.

I stopped again to rest.

Ahead the sand sloped downward where thickened clumps of grass marked a small stream. As I heaved slightly for breath, a stray part of my mind marked the single set of deer tracks that veered in from the left and made sharps points down to the stream.

I took a step forward.

A silent alarm bell triggered inside.

The deer tracks.

Weird. They just ended. As if a giant hawk had swooped down and picked it clean.

I shook off the alarm.

Another step.

Then a cold sweat.

What if . . .

I stepped backward and found a heavy piece of wood.

I tossed it a foot beyond where the deer tracks ended.

My sweat went from a chill to ice.

The wood tilted and slowly sank.

Quicksand!

I could hear Ralphy's voice explaining how sometimes water bubbled upward beneath the sand, holding the particles suspended in an illusion of solidness.

I fought a shudder at thinking how the deer must have struggled, with terror-widened nostrils straining for sky, until the sand soundlessly closed over to leave no trace of the unwary.

Thank you, God, I whispered for not having taken the next, fatal step.

My knees were still weak as I looked for and found a fallen sapling, then stripped it of branches. I would use it as a pole to test the ground ahead of me at every step. And, should that fail, I would turn it sideways to catch the edges of solid ground.

Another deep breath before moving ahead, careful to skirt the patch of quicksand by at least a dozen yards.

How to keep a straight line of direction?

Then it hit me.

Sight on something unusual—a lightning-torched tree or a gap in the branches. Then sight on something ahead of that. Keep them both in line. Reach the first object, then sight for a third object beyond the second. Keep them in line until reaching the second object. Sight a fourth beyond the third. And so on.

It became a monotony.

Scramble over logs. Fight through bramble. Accept the sandy soil patches between with gratitude.

What kept me going was discovering my guess had been correct. There were few swamps or marshes along the way. In other words, we weren't in airboat country. The Everglade swamps did not surround us in all directions.

I have to hit a road sometime.

Two hours passed.

Then, in the middle of the haze of sweat mixed with the blood of scratches and slapped mosquitoes, I stepped onto another fallen log and balanced for a moment before stepping down.

As my right foot dropped, I saw it. The blur of movement that was the rising head of a snake.

And it was much too late to stop.

I froze there. Right foot on the ground. Left foot up on the log behind me, leg bent upward at a painful angle. I was far too off balance to consider using my quicksand pole as a baseball bat for protection.

I teetered and sucked in a lungful of air.

The snake's head wavered as it stared with flat eyes of night. Gray brown splotches like fallen leaves draped a thick body at least five feet long.

I did not breathe.

I started to lose my balance.

The snake reared its head back.

For me, it was either fall forward or fling my arms out to stabilize and startle the snake with sudden movement.

It seemed like a freeze-frame motion. My arms started outward and the pole whirred in the air. The snake snapped its jaws open, wide as a steel trap.

In that horribly slow movement of time, I registered only one thing. The inside of the snake's mouth was pale milk white.

Cottonmouth!

The giant head arched forward.

I might have screamed, but there was no way to hear. Because the roar of an explosion sucked all sound from my lungs, and the head of the snake simply disappeared.

CHAPTER 19

Ten minutes later I was in the shade of a screened porch at the front of a sturdy cabin almost hidden beneath the spread of large oaks.

It was difficult not to stare at the headless body of the cottonmouth where it hung on a nail from the edge of the railings. My rescuer handed me a tall glass of lemonade and pointed at the snake for emphasis.

"Son," he said, "if I hadn't come along when I did, and if I didn't have my shotgun like I did, you'd be a sick puppy by now. That's one big daddy of a cottonmouth. Venom from that snake, well, it doesn't work like others. Nope, the poison just dissolves all body tissue. It would've pumped you full of juice and your blood vessels would have turned to spaghetti. Ten minutes later—"

"Thank you, sir."

He raised a bushy gray eyebrow in irritation for being interrupted.

"I mean for the lemonade," I said quickly.

The man in front of me grumped a few times, deep in the back of his throat. His bushy eyebrows matched his thick, almost white hair. His face was broad and handsome but was starting to sag at the cheeks and below his chin, like a fading movie star. A sweat-stained, checked flannel shirt covered wide shoulders and a large belly. He wore khaki pants and high, laced leather boots.

He changed the grumping in his throat to a gruff question. "Any fool knows not to step over a log into shade, especially near water. It's exactly where a cottonmouth will be cooling itself. What were you doing out there, anyway?"

Two gulps of life-saving lemonade. I gasped at the pleasure of that cool liquid before speaking.

"That's what I was trying to tell you, sir. Looking for a road. We were kidnapped and—"

He held up a gnarled and callused hand.

"Son, I used to be in the Bureau. Practical jokes don't amuse me. And talk of kidnapping is serious business. That's why I brought you here first. To give your head a chance to clear."

I turned red remembering how ten minutes ago I had babbled gratitude and excitement to realize that someone had shot the snake a split second before it could slash forward into my leg.

"My head *is* clear. At least now, sir. There's an island back there in Moonshiner's Bay. Guarded by Big Ben. And my brother and a friend are waiting with a cooler of food for me to find a road and—"

"Slow down, son, You're getting that look in your eyes again."

I slowed down and explained. Everything.

He listened carefully, but that didn't stop him from reaching over to grab the body of the snake. He pulled a folding knife from his pocket, tested the blade for sharpness with the back of his thumbnail, and began skinning the snake.

Instead of watching him cut apart the snake, I decided it would be better to study the rough wooden floorboards as I told my story. From when the cops kidnapped us from Disney World to Joel and the skunk to six slaps on the water for Big Ben to crossing the pond. I didn't tell him about crying on the water, though.

"Clem Pickett? Hostage for a coin you know nothing about?" he asked. "And they called the swamp Moonshiner's Bay?"

"Yes, sir."

He stopped his work on the snake and watched me gravely with pale blue eyes almost hidden by those big eyebrows. "Son, there's only one problem with all of this."

"Sir?"

"I've been here the last twenty years. Ask anybody. They'll tell you that Blake Hotridge—that's me—knows the country about as well as anyone. And I've never heard of any place called Moonshiner's Bay."

I told myself that we were doing the best thing possible for Joel and Lisa. But it still didn't feel right to be riding in the cab of a pickup truck and heading away from the swamp and bush that held them prisoner.

I didn't have much choice. Not with Blake Hotridge directing the operation.

"Couple more miles of this dirt track," he said without looking over. "Then Rock Ridge Road, then Number 85 north to Dade City. We'll get all this straightened out there."

I had a feeling his definition of straightened out meant proving my story wrong.

"You don't believe me, do you, Mr. Hotridge?"

He still didn't look over. "It's not that, son. I told you. There's no way you could find your way back to your friends. I don't know what island you're talking about. So we've got to get hold of a county map to see if this Moonshiner's Bay is called something else. And it might not be a bad idea to call your folks and maybe the people you left behind in Disney World. And, of course, the police."

"Yes, sir." Still, I wondered if he was more concerned about confirming my story than looking for Lisa and Joel.

Blake drove carefully to avoid most of the potholes.

To break the silence, I tried small talk.

"You mentioned the 'bureau,' sir?"

He caught the lack of comprehension in my voice.

"Bureau. FBI. Federal Bureau of Investigation."

I whistled in appreciation of an exciting job like that.

"It's not like that," Blake said. "It's a tiring job. Too much grind. And

I wanted out. My wife died only a few years after we were married, and I had no kids to worry about. Life was simpler here and land was cheap. Cheap enough for me to retire early."

That explained his lack of accent. Another transplant into Florida.

"I get into town whenever I need supplies," he said. "But for the most part I value the quiet out there. And I like trying to be self-sufficient."

That explained the snake skinning. He'd hung the strips of skin to dry and thrown the meat of the snake to a pig kept in a small pen behind his shack.

Something about his tone told me he also valued quiet in the cab of his truck. I said nothing else, and he didn't seem upset by that at all.

Half an hour later we reached the outskirts of Dade City, a small town east some eighty miles—as a map in the glove compartment showed—by highway from Orlando.

It was two o'clock Wednesday afternoon. If it took two hours to track our way back to Moonshiner's Bay, and another hour to return, and two more hours to reach Orlando, Lisa and Joel and I could be back in time for a late supper.

We'd let the police sort out the rest. Or so I thought.

CHAPTER 20

The quiet streets and wide sidewalks and tall shade trees and square wood houses of Dade City made it feel as if I were stepping back into a timeless summer. I half expected to see Model T Fords in the driveways and along the curbs.

The downtown area—maybe a dozen square blocks—had few steel-and-concrete buildings. Instead, one- and two-story weathered brick stores and banks added serenity to the scene.

I would have relaxed if I could.

But Lisa and Joel and his stupid teddy bear had already been alone for the last too many hours. Would Blake Hotridge be able to guess at my erratic path through the woods?

He had explained it earlier by telling me I could not have traveled more than ten miles in my two-hour walk. All we needed to find was a body of water with an island somewhere in a ten-mile circle around his cabin. A body of water reachable by airboat. Then we'd go back—by boat—and bring Lisa and Joel back to civilization.

I glanced at the sun as its brightness bounced through the dusty windshield.

Mr. Hotridge read my mind.

"Don't worry, son. We've got at least four hours of daylight left."

He braked for an old lady who stepped onto the street without looking in either direction. At the sound of our slowing tires, she looked up and smiled sweetly from behind old-fashioned cat-eye glasses.

"I love small towns," he said as she hobbled across with the help of a cane. "No one's in a hurry. Especially Mrs. Hart."

I was. But I didn't say so.

Mr. Hotridge slowly accelerated, then two blocks later cranked the steering wheel to turn into a shaded parking lot.

"Here we are," he said. "We'll kill two birds with one stone and get a search party organized a lot quicker."

"Sir?"

He pointed at a sign beside a flagpole.

"Sheriff's office. He'll have a detailed map. And you can tell him about the kidnapping."

"Oh."

Mr. Hotridge shifted into park and turned to look at me squarely for the first time since leaving his cabin. "I believe you, of course. The sheriff might not."

I waited.

"It should be easy, though, to prove your story true," Mr. Hotridge continued. "All you have to do is point out which prisoner is Clem Pickett."

"Sheriff Leroy," Mr. Hotridge called loudly as he swung open the thick wooden doors that led into the cool corridor, "we got here a boy who says he's been kidnapped."

I heard the sound of a chair spinning on its wheels ahead, where sunshine poured in through windows.

"Git outer here. That you, Blake?"

We kept walking as Mr. Hotridge answered. "This here boy—Ricky Kidd—has got a claim we need to substantiate."

The sheriff stepped out from a small office with a large glass window.

He reached the counter that separated us, leaned forward on massive elbows, and looked down on me.

No one else was on the straight-backed bench seats in the foyer. Except for the rustling of papers in a smaller office beside the sheriff's, it was quiet. No ringing of telephones. No static of police radios. A nice, sleepy small town.

"Sub-stan-she-ate?" The thick accent told me this man had not been born anywhere else but here.

"Yes," Mr. Hotridge said heavily. "Verify. Make true."

Sheriff Leroy chuckled. It was an action that made his double chin wobble in all directions. His eyes were deeply burrowed behind the huge pockets of flesh that entirely hid his cheekbones. His green gray shirt was big enough to set up in the backyard and sleep three.

"Whenever I kin, I test Mr. Hotridge here," he drawled. "A courtesy from one ol' FBI boy to 'nother, to keep him sharp."

I nodded. All I wanted was for the search to begin.

"So." The sheriff turned his attention to Mr. Hotridge. "What story needs *sub-stan-she-ating*, and how do y'awl propose we do it?"

Point by point, Mr. Hotridge summed up everything I had told him. He didn't miss a thing, leaving me awed by the detailed precision that must have been a habit during his FBI days.

Sheriff Leroy sniffed. "Boy, I don't mean to be insulting, but you do smell as if you bin out in the woods fer a few days."

I hadn't thought of that. I mean, I did feel dirty and worn out, but it didn't seem important with what I had to worry about.

"Sorry, sir," I began.

Sheriff Leroy waved a big hand in my direction. "Ain't your fault."

He studied Blake Hotridge's face, as if to see if *he* was pulling a prank.

"Hostage for a coin. If that don't beat all," the sheriff repeated thoughtfully. "Sounds interesting. But I don't reckon Clem'll say much. He's been awful quiet of late."

Mr. Hotridge shrugged. "You got what—four, five men in the holding cells? If the boy makes an ID on Pickett, we know this is serious enough to send a couple men out."

Sheriff Leroy drummed his fingers on the counter top. "Reckon it'd be a real waste of time if the kid's jest a-talking." He stopped strumming. "But dad blast it, we cain't take a chance and leave two other young'uns out thar amongst the skeeters and gators...."

It was a weird feeling to be standing there with them talking around me as if I were a puppy on a leash.

Sheriff Leroy made his decision.

"Clovis!" Sheriff Leroy bellowed. "Y'ain't done a lick a' work all day!"

A deputy sheriff in a matching green gray uniform appeared from the other small office, yawning and stretching. I recognized him as one of the two cops who had arrested Clem at the airport the day we arrived in Orlando.

"Take this here boy to the cells," Sheriff Leroy said to Clovis. "Have him nod when he reaches Clem Pickett. Unnerstand? No talk. Pickett's crookeder than a washtub of snakes, and I don't want him influencing a material witness."

Sheriff Leroy smiled down on me. "Sounds important, don't it? Material witness."

He then waved me away and, like a portable backstop, retreated his huge body back to his office.

There were five men in the three cells at the back of the building.

It took less than a minute to walk through and exactly three seconds to identify Clem Pickett. Only because he was so big. Not because his face looked the same.

He sat on the edge of his bed, staring blankly ahead at the steel bars between us. The walrus mustache, once full and proud, was bedraggled with dirt and sweat. His hair was matted, his eyes dull. Blue-yellow bruises swelled one side of his face.

The deputy caught my expression of surprise.

"That ol' boy fell down the stairs," he explained. "Hurt his face real good."

Clem did not look up. He spoke from the side of his mouth with no expression in his voice. "Funny how Leroy has stairs armed with fists, Clovis."

Clovis began to push me on. "Sheriff Leroy tole us he'd be a-lying."

Clem Pickett raised his eyes and focused on me for the first time. He flinched with recognition, then jumped to his feet.

Clovis pushed me harder, but I strained to look back over my shoulder at Clem.

Clem reached the bars and grabbed them with both hands.

"Boy," he cried. "Run! First chance you git. Run like a rabbit!"

The steel doors clanged as Clovis pulled me through.

"Folks call him crazy," Clovis said with a disgusted shake of his head. " 'Course, any man who murders his uncle's got more than a bolt or two loose."

I followed and could think of no reply.

We reached the foyer, where Blake Hotridge was waiting.

"Postive ID, Clovis?"

"Yep. The boy spotted him real quick. 'Course, Clem started a pack a' lies jest as quick."

Mr. Hotridge snorted. "Figures."

Then he put a hand on my shoulder. "Sorry to doubt you, son. But now we'll get a full search going."

He called into the sheriff's office. "Leroy, we need a map and two men!"

Sheriff Leroy stuck his head out the door. "Two men? Blake, I got one man called in sick."

Mr. Hotridge had no time to reply to the sheriff. Just then someone shuffled in through the front door.

The old lady in cat-eye glasses.

"Why, Mrs. Hart," Mr. Hotridge said. "If I had only known you were headed this way, I would certainly have given you a lift."

"That's kind of you," the old lady said. "No harm done."

She swiveled to look at the sheriff. "Unlike the damage one of your deputies has done to my boardinghouse."

"Ma'am?" Sheriff Leroy said.

"Next time he gets sprayed on duty, you can just send him to a motel until the smell wears away. My every room smells like a week-old cat. It's hardly worth the bother of renting to him. And I don't know why you don't let animal control take care of skunks, anyway."

What a coincidence, I began to think. *Two grown men in the same week getting sprayed . . .*

Then I noticed the other deputy—the one who had taken me back to the cell area—staring at me. A cat intent on a mouse. As if wondering if I would realize the danger ready to pounce.

And suddenly Clem Pickett's croaked and desperate advice minutes earlier made sense.

My feet churned against the smooth floor. I ducked around the old lady and hit full speed as I crashed through the doors and into the sunlight.

CHAPTER 21

A stranger in a strange town, with cops in full pursuit.

I didn't even have time to think about it. It was *run, baby, run.* Anything not to be near Sheriff Leroy or his deputies.

I had two things in my favor. A two-minute head start. And years of practice avoiding Joel. Compared to him, overweight and out-of-shape small-town cops were a breeze.

I pulled the old pizza parlor trick—in the front and out the back.

That gave me a screen—the building. Once in the alley, I had three directions to choose: ahead, left, or right. I cut left.

A hundred yards later I added the old double-back routine. Joel would have sneered at the simplicity. But I was sure it was enough to fool these cops. So I cut left again through another store and came back out onto the same street I had crossed in leaving the sheriff's office.

I checked both ways before dashing across the street, slowed to a hasty stride, and entered a department store on the other side.

With Joel, I'd only have a thirty-second cushion of safety. Here, I figured I had just bought myself five minutes.

But I needed a more permanent escape. More time to think. And more time to ask questions.

Four minutes and fifty seconds left.

I ignored the surly glances of a bored salesclerk and made

sure that a clothing rack hid me from the entrance of the department store. My heart verged on a panic attack.

Four minutes and forty seconds left.

What to do?

I made sure there was an exit at the back of the store.

Four minutes and thirty seconds left.

A dress from the clothing rack brushed against my face as I peered out at the street.

Four minutes and twenty seconds.

The dress brushed my face again.

Then a painful thought hit me. I patted my back pocket. Yes, I still had my wallet, one filled with enough money for an entire vacation.

Four minutes and ten seconds—at the most—until cops arrive to check out this side of the street.

The painful thought grew more painful.

Four minutes and five seconds.

I surrendered to the thought. And sighed.

The only person in Dade City able to help was still alive. She answered the door of a small cottage near the edge of town before I needed to knock twice.

"Begging yo' pardon, missy," she said with a twinkle, "but you are flat-out the ugliest girl chile I ever laid my eyes upon."

"May I come in, Mrs. Pickett? I'm the person who called you twenty minutes ago."

She waved her hanky in front of her nose. "And, chile, you smell worse'n a dead polecat. Thass no way to be sellin' magazine subscriptions or cookie boxes from one door to the next."

I looked nervously behind me for the sheriff's men.

"I'm not selling, ma'am. It's a matter of life or death. And it's about Clem."

The old lady searched my eyes. She must have found truth, because she pulled me in and shut the door.

"You fine, chile?"

I shook my head in misery. The dress was rubbing my shoulders raw. The high-heeled shoes had already given me blisters. And I had nearly fainted three times from the heat of wearing a wig.

She pointed at a high-backed red velvet chair in the front room.

"Set your behind down and rest a spell. I'll bring some iced tea."

When she returned, I had already taken off the wig and set it on the rug in front of my chair.

She smiled. "Honey chile, I'm a-crowdin' eighty years, and I always hankered to be blond, jest once. How was it?"

I could not help but smile in return. This was one tough old woman. How many others would open the door to find a boy dressed as a girl and make jokes about it?

She waited until I had drained the last of the iced tea. And she waited until I explained.

I told her how I'd purchased the clothing and wig, then gone back into the street—not yet in disguise—to let the sheriff's men spot me again. The last thing I wanted was them checking the department store and asking questions to discover what I had purchased. Then, as Ricky Kidd, I'd dodged them again, found a deserted spot, and changed into the dress and shoes. That had given me enough time to plan the next few hours. And time to call all the Picketts in the phone book to find Clem's mother.

"Have you called your folks?" Mrs. Pickett asked. "That'd seem like the most logical thing to do from here."

I shook my head. "Not yet. They're too far away. They can't do anything, and I don't want to drive them crazy with worry. Not if they can't call the police to step in. I decided to come here first."

Mrs. Pickett nodded, then stared at me thoughtfully. "That's twice now you mention you cain't trust the sheriff's men. And we still ain't got around to why you and Clem is in this."

So, again, I found myself giving an explanation from the beginning. Meeting Clem on the airplane. The kidnapping. The blindfolded airboat ride. The demand for a coin I hadn't seen.

While I spoke, her eyes never left my face. She had brilliant white hair, wrapped in a tight bun at the top of her head. Her bifocals slipped each time she nodded and rocked in her wooden chair but never fell from her nose. She left her hands folded quietly in the lap of her dress and, despite my story, seemed as relaxed as if we were discussing the weather.

"Tell me, son," she finally spoke near the end, "why was it you fled the sheriff's office?"

"A few things," I began. "All of them point to Sheriff Leroy and his deputies as our kidnappers."

She stiffened, barely enough to notice.

"Sheriff Leroy made a big deal of not letting me talk to Clem. *Then* he said it was because Clem was a liar. *Now* I think it's because he knew Clem would try to warn me."

Mrs. Pickett pursed her lips. The wrinkles on her face ran upward, as if she had spent much of her life with smiles in place.

"That's assumin' a whole bunch," she said.

Long shadows across the floor suddenly reminded me how quickly time was passing. And how urgently I needed help and information from this woman.

"The biggest clue was the skunk," I said. "Remember I told you that Joel had managed to get one of our kidnappers sprayed? When I heard that one of the deputies had been sprayed by a skunk—and saw how the deputy at the sheriff's office stared at me—I knew the other deputy was that kidnapper. Both of them Sheriff Leroy's men."

Mrs. Pickett let out a long and sad sigh. "I was a-feared o' that."

"Ma'am?"

"Leroy 'tain't the sheriff's *last* name."

I didn't understand.

She lifted one of her delicate hands from her lap and rubbed her forehead as if to ease pain.

"You see, the sheriff's last name is Pickett. You unnerstand now? Sheriff Leroy Pickett. He's my oldest boy, Clem's elder brother."

CHAPTER 22

"Where's a body to begin?" she asked seconds later. "Fifteen years a' hatred needs a pile of explainin'."

"The coin?" I replied.

She waved a fluttery hand at me. "Durn stupidity, the legend behind those coins. Clem's granpappy never should'a started the tomfoolery."

"Legend?" I echoed. "Coins? Grandfather?"

She waved again. Less flutter and more disgust.

"Clem's granpappy—my long-dead husband's pappy, bless both their departed souls. They say the ol' man cut his fortune in corn likker—that's shine, moonshine. But I never believed a word. And the legend ain't important to what happened betwixt Clem and Leroy."

I itched. I stank. I was on the run. Joel and Lisa were marooned on an island in a swamp guarded by a monster alligator. And I had to sit politely and wait for the story to unfold at the old lady's own pace.

Worse, she began to excuse herself from the front room. "I'll get my book a' clippin's and photos. And I see you could certainly use another batch of iced tea. Won't be but a minute."

While she was gone, I quietly drew the drapes shut. It felt terrible to be on the run. And I hadn't done anything wrong.

I sat again.

The front room held little else to distract me from my itching, smelliness, impatience, and fear. It was wallpapered in a simple striped pattern. Nothing in furniture aside from her rocking chair, my easy chair, and an empty coffee table. A pile of magazines was stacked neatly in one corner. It was definitely not a room she spent much time in.

My mind turned back to the new information. Clem's grandfather had been a moonshiner. Some believed he had made a fortune doing it. Some didn't. That meant if there really was a fortune, no one had found it. Otherwise, everyone would believe he had a fortune. So if the coins were wanted badly enough to lead to a kidnapping, they must be related to this unknown or undiscovered fortune. But how would a coin or coins—

"More tea," her voice interrupted my thoughts, "and some pictures of mighty fine young men."

Mrs. Pickett put the glass into my hand, then pulled her rocker up near my chair and spread open a scrapbook in her lap.

She flipped through slowly, with a half hum of words and names to herself as she did.

I sipped my tea and watched her thin hands perform the ritual of moving through the scrapbook.

Black-and-white photos with curled edges. Color snapshots fading to yellow. Newspaper clippings. And beneath every one, neat handwriting in blue ink.

She found the page she wanted.

"A gradge-ee-ation article. Right there."

I tried to scan it, but the scrapbook wavered too much in her hands. All I could be sure of was the headline of the short article: LEROY PICKETT, FBI GRAD.

"I was fit to bust with pride that day," Mrs. Pickett said softly. "My own boy. And his first assignment was back home where all us folks could see what he'd done."

Across from the first page was a barely recognizable man standing beneath a strangely familiar tree with a very recognizable man. Behind them, water.

I steadied the scrapbook with my left hand and pointed with my right hand. "That's Mr. Hotridge," I said. "Who's with him?"

"Leroy. They was fresh from up north and the academy school. That was before Leroy got sloppy and stopped a-caring 'bout his weight."

The sadness in her voice told me not to ask for an explanation.

She turned to the next page and pointed to another photo.

"Leroy again. Like a buck in the prime of life. Beside him, the boy what thought the sun set and rose on big brother Leroy."

I didn't have to ask.

It was Clem Pickett. Much younger, of course, and without his walrus mustache. Arm around Leroy, half embarrassed to be caught in a brotherly hug. Again, behind them, that strangely familiar tree.

"And Leroy?" She spoke to herself more than me. "He loved Clem mighty fierce. They was close 'cause their pappy died so young. Leroy always wanted nothing but the best for Clem."

A twist of pain made me flinch. *Even if Joel drives me nuts, he's an okay brother, but now he's stuck out there and . . .*

"So it took all the wind right outta Leroy's sails when he had to arrest Clem for murder. Like Leroy gave up on life right there. Ate, drank, and smoked until folks could hardly tell him apart from a bear."

"It is true?" I asked. "About why Clem was sent to jail? He murdered his uncle?"

Mrs. Pickett arched her back straight as a post and jutted her jaw forward. "Clem was found guilty a' murder. That ain't saying he *done* it. Jest that he got blamed."

I nodded, but it was too late. Her nostalgic mood of fond memories was gone.

She snapped the scrapbook shut. "That says it, now, don't it? One brother set against t'other. Lawman a-hating the jailbird. A-hating him 'nuff to throw him back in jail as soon as he arrived home. And you in the middle for some coin that already caused two generations of bad blood."

I was about to ask her what we could do next when it dawned on me. The tree. And the water behind it.

Those photos were taken on the island that now holds Lisa and Joel!

"Ma'am," I began quietly, "exactly where were Leroy and Mr. Hotridge in that one photo?"

She didn't have to reopen the scrapbook to say. I expect she had every page and every photo memorized.

"Moonshiner's Bay." That even brought a chuckle from her. "Not the water, a' course. Thass no bay. Jest a swamp. But folks called the *island* Moonshiner's Bay. Everyone back then knew it held Clem's granpappy's still. Joke was that a person crazy 'nuff to drink his corn likker'd be crazy 'nuff to bay at the moon."

I nearly bounced with excitement. "That's where Lisa and my brother are! Can we get there tonight?"

She smiled sweetly and patted her thighs. "Not on these old legs."

I probably showed every nerve ending of disappointment. *Who else can I trust among these strangers?*

Then she patted my knee. "Son, ain't no reason to be downhearted. I'm a-taking you to the folks what know the swamps best and hate Sheriff Leroy the most."

I tried to smile in return.

"Yes, sir," she said. "Ain't nobody got cause to hate me and Leroy more'n the family whose pappy was kilt by Clem. They ain't spoke to me or Leroy since."

CHAPTER 23

"Chile, it could be real bad instead a' jest moderate bad."

I wondered how much worse it could be, about to be abandoned at the end of a narrow road in the growing dark with the glowing yellow lights of the only human habitation in sight belonging to the mobile home of a family that had hated Clem Pickett for the last fifteen years.

"This ain't—I mean isn't—real bad?" I asked.

"Bad? I'll tell you bad. Bad is having a crooked sheriff for a son. Bad is having yo' other boy known as a convicted killer. Bad is having 'em both hate each other 'nuff to have innercent chillren like you caught betwixt. And bad is havin' to turn to folks what you been feudin' with for fifteen years and ask them to cause grief for your oldest boy, jest to rescue them innercent chillren. Now, that's bad."

Which didn't leave me much to say above the purring of the engine as she slowed to a stop.

She chortled in a low voice way across the seat of her massive and almost antique Chevrolet.

" 'Course, I'm too old not to know that unless'n you look at the funny side a' life, it ain't worth livin'. So I'll tell you what's real bad."

A funny side to this?

"At least you don't have to show up at folks like these folks inna dress. Now, that'd be real bad."

Great. My only consolation as I approached a shackful of alligator poachers would be that I now wore my smelly old jeans and T-shirt instead of a dress.

"Thank you, ma'am," I forced myself to say, "for stopping near the park to let me pick up my clothes."

"No thanks needed. Jest git your friends rescued," Mrs. Pickett said, switching back to an almost grim tone. "Then do two things."

"Yes?"

"Let this trouble betwixt Leroy and Clem sort itself out. You stay away. Unnerstand?"

"Yes."

"And the second thing." Another chortle. "Git yourself a bath as soon as possible. I never believed a person could smell as bad as you."

I stood there shivering, as the twilight faded into soft purple, for five minutes after the Chevrolet's taillights disappeared in distance and dust.

It was not cold that made me shiver. Far from it. The Florida air—with the sun now gone—seemed warm and friendly instead of furnace-blasting harsh.

No, I shivered from fear. Mrs. Pickett had driven me away from Dade City back in the direction of the isolated gator country I had left only hours earlier.

I knew from the map in Mr. Hotridge's glove compartment that huge tracts of the land nearby consisted of dozens and dozens of square miles of wildlife management area, broken only by rough, four-wheel-drive trails.

I also knew—from Mrs. Pickett—that the Johnsons scratched a living here on the edge of that land. And they weren't too concerned about the law in doing it—poaching was the nicest of the things they did.

But if the Johnsons were the ones who could mount a nighttime operation to rescue Joel and Lisa from the swamp, then I would have to be the one to walk forward and knock on their door.

I took my first step.

And froze at a stab in my lower back.

"What I got pokin' in yo' back be the business end."

"Yes, sir!" I said instantly. It didn't feel like a feather duster.

"And being as I got a real itchy finger on the trigger end, my advice is that you be mighty particular about choosing the right words t'explain yo'self and yo' presence hereby."

I would have gulped if my mouth had had any more moisture than a desert in a windstorm. "I wasn't trying to be sneaky, sir. I mean, nobody gets dropped off from a car if they're trying to be sneaky."

Another nudge in my back. "Who all dropped you off?"

I felt like biting my tongue in two for such a stupid way to start. If this was a Johnson—and who else could be quiet enough to materialize like that—he wouldn't be happy to hear the Pickett name.

"Who?" Another nudge came with the question.

"A . . . a . . . a lady who said you had, um, cause not to support Sheriff Leroy."

He grunted. "Mighty smart lady. What be her name?"

"Mrs. Eunice Pickett."

A pause. Long enough for a dozen mosquitoes to attack my neck. Not that I dared move to swat them flat.

Finally he spoke. "Walk ahead, son. Real slow till we get to them porch lights. My feelin' is I'm about to hear a whopper of a tale."

CHAPTER 24

They crowded onto a lopsided porch that was an after-thought to the mobile home, more of them than I could count in the dimness, and within moments I realized that it *was* possible to exude more of a campy smell than I did.

Raw, untamed country kids, all of them with the sullenness of wild cats. And the smell.

Not that I planned to recommend city life while that shotgun hung loose in the crook of the man's arm. He wore a greasy baseball cap, and I could not read any expression in the shadows of his face.

He burped carelessly and waved his free hand at the brood of children around us.

"Boy, whatever story you got, you might as well tell alla us."

I told it yet one more time. From the kidnapping to the coin to the island with Lisa and Joel to Sheriff Leroy.

This Johnson man cocked his head slightly to listen, and I felt rather than saw the intensity of his stare from beneath the shadow of his cap.

Halfway through my story, it dawned on me that all of his children were extremely quiet and well behaved. I regretted whatever disdainful nose sniffing I had done in silence on my arrival.

"I was right," the man said to himself. "That story were a whopper."

"You don't believe me, sir? You're my last hope."

"Tain't a matter of belief. Jest takes a while to settle, a tale that big."

Great.

I was quite sure the sheriff and his men would leave Joel and Lisa on the island all night. They had no reason to believe I would be able to find anyone who knew about its location and even less reason to believe I'd find someone to lead me there in the dark. But without the help from this silent and suspicious man, I had nowhere else to turn. And then a few hours into tomorrow's daylight—long enough for the sheriff to arrive and move them—Lisa and Joel might be anywhere in the tangled Florida backwoods.

"Elmer." A quiet, strong voice broke into my thoughts.

I nearly jumped to notice it came from a woman not much bigger than the tallest of the children. His wife?

"Yes'm."

"Elmer, you know the boy ain't lying. Listen to how he talks. He ain't local. There ain't no other way for him to know about Clem and Leroy and the island and the coins and such unless all that stuff really did happen."

"Yes'm."

Elmer sounded glum.

"Well?"

"Yes'm. 'Tis my Christian duty to help out any an' all in distress."

"Then quit a-dragging your feet. This boy shows more distress than a coon what's been treed. Stand tall and tell 'im you'll take 'im tonight. You're the only one in this here country that kin."

Silence from Elmer.

Then he grabbed his cap by its bill and slapped his leg before grinning. "It don't hurt none to think about the pain I might cause Sheriff Leroy, either."

I grinned back, then jumped about a foot when he twirled the shotgun in a quick movement, pointed it at the roof of the porch, and pulled the trigger.

Only an empty click.

"Jest funnin', boy. Think any Johnson'd need to use a loaded gun on some fella from the city?"

"Elmer," his wife chuckled. "Y'alla's been a show-off."

I never did see her face clearly before leaving. Or get a chance to thank her.

"Clem Pickett kilt my pappy over one a' them moonshine coins," Elmer said matter-of-factly as we followed a path through the woods that led away from his mobile home.

I had been relieved, as we headed into the darkness and mosquitoes, to see him pop five shells into the breech of his shotgun. And I was even more relieved when he offered me some stinky, gooey insect repellent, the pride in his voice evident as he told me it was homemade. By then, of course, I didn't care how bad I smelled.

"You're first cousins to Clem, right? Your father was Clem's uncle?"

"Thass right, boy."

He stopped and turned to me. The flashlight in his hand dangled at his side and pointed at the grass. Heavy dew droplets sparkled tiny diamonds of light back up at us.

"This is the story, son. My maw and his pappy were the only two chillren of ol' Madman Charlie, my granpappy. He got his name on account of nobody in their right mind'd mess with him and his likker business. He was so good, in fact, common talk said he made enough shine to float a ferry. Folks hold he made pert near a million before Prohibition 'twere over."

I nodded.

"Trouble was, the Feds started sniffin' round like dogs on a coon trail. Ol' Madman, he was tough, but even he knew not to mess with the Feds. Some say he buried his money. Some say it was jest a legend. Whatever it were, he jest laid low. Never spent a dime."

Elmer Johnson's voice had slipped into the cadence of a good storyteller. He wove a spell with words, and as he spoke, I forgot how urgently we needed to get to Moonshiner's Bay.

"Come time to die for ol' Madman Charlie—some folks held he was too tough for even that—he called Clem's pappy and my maw to his death-bed. They were hardly more'n children. Gave 'em each a coin."

I could see this man telling the story across a campfire to his children, with the same Florida moon that now rose for us as a backdrop for them, too.

"Jest one coin each," Elmer continued. "Tole 'em both it were their inheritance. That putting both coins together might show them more money than twinkling stars."

Elmer paused, as if he was satisfied to be telling the story the way it was always told.

"Condition was," he began again, "they couldn't show them coins each t'other. Not till the boy—who would become Clem's pappy—was twenty-one, old enough to outsmart any Feds that might still be waiting."

I coughed to clear my throat before speaking, that's how reluctant I was to break his spell in the warm night air. "The Feds were still hanging around all those years?"

Elmer grinned. "Naw. They got fancier ways to nab a fella now. Income tax. Say you move into a fancy house but got no means a' support, they come sniffin' around all over again."

"Oh."

"Anyways," Elmer said, "Clem's pappy got to be pert near twenty years old. He got married, first had Leroy, then got hisself called to the Korean War, and Clem was born whilst he was over thar." A short pause while Elmer placed his cap over his heart. "Clem's pappy never did come back."

Cap back on his head. "That left my maw with her coin, God rest her soul. When she got married, she gave it to Pappy, a Johnson. Didn't do no good, not with the other one gone."

Elmer sighed. "Then one day word got out that Leroy had the other coin, that his daddy had left it behind as a keepsake. Once Leroy was growed some, my own pappy tried to sweet-talk him outta it. T'weren't a good thing to do, and my pappy regretted his moment a' weakness what caused Leroy to never trust him since. It went on for years, each having the other half of the key to a fortune, and each refusing to show it t'other."

Elmer shook his head. "Then came the day—it were rainin' real good—that Sheriff Leroy, now long growed up, got a tip that something real bad were happening out by Moonshiner's Bay. He got out there jest in time to catch Clem with blood on his hands, gittin' in a boat. Sheriff Leroy goes back to the shack and finds my pappy's wallet and fav-o-right fishing knife in the dirt, more blood all over, and heel marks like a body's been dragged to the water."

Elmer shook his head again, and this time his voice lost its soft story-telling quality and began to fill with hate. "Boy, all anybody could figure was that Clem kilt my pappy for the coin—maybe so's to match it with Leroy's later. But nobody never found the coin on him, and Clem, he jest shut right up, never said another word, even at the trial."

I thought of the giant man, how gentle he had been talking to Joel on the plane. The way his head was bowed as he sat in the Dade City Jail. I protested on his behalf. "Clem admitted he did it?"

"Nope. Clem never said nothin' all through the trial. Jest sat there like stone. Not one yes. Not one no. Didn't even blink when they sentenced him to all them years up north to the pen. Law says iffen the body cain't be found—and it weren't, not in that gator pond—a person cain't prove murder. Iffen Clem even talked a'tall, folks hold, he'd 'a been released. But the jury figured the blood and the wallet were 'nuff clues and Clem's silence was 'nuff admission a' guilt."

I could think of nothing to say. And, like Dad always says, don't put your mouth in gear unless it's got a place to go. So the croaking of distant frogs and the rustlings in the dark velvet air were the only noises around us.

Then Elmer sighed. "I loved my pappy," he said. "Always figured life mighta been different with him around. Maybe I'd 'a found a job instead a' always looking for the easy way, the way past the law, what with poaching and all."

He said nothing more, just turned and began walking again.

The beam of his flashlight poked and prodded at the darkness, and we followed the twisted path until we reached water.

The light of his flashlight found the side of his aluminum boat.

"Generally," Elmer said, "iffen I need to be out there at night, I head out during daylight. Safer, and nobody pays attention to the noise. Tonight, though, it 'pears important enough not to worry 'bout waking the law. In and out, thass the way it'll be."

There was a slight scuffling of bushes near the boat.

" 'Fraid it won't, Elmer."

Two men. The same rubber masks as before. Except this time, each man cradled a shotgun.

Elmer didn't faint with fright, so I barely managed to do the same.

"You don't appear to be no welcomin' committee at no debutante ball," Elmer commented. "This mean I ain't making a midnight run?"

"On the contrary," Rubber Mask Number One said. "You're going, all right. We jest wanna join you and the boy for the ride."

CHAPTER 25

We arrived after twenty-five minutes of foam churning white behind the boat in the moonlit, inky black water. Elmer cut the engine and timed the final coast into land so perfectly that the bow of the boat barely nudged shore as it stopped.

"Folks got it right," Rubber Mask Number One said in the relief of silence. "Ain't nobody else could get a body here in the dark of night but Elmer Johnson."

"Thass right," Mask Number Two chuckled. "Which is exactly why we was waiting where we was. You'd be the only one to turn to iffen the boy had his plans fer rescue."

Elmer said nothing in return, only stared back with eyes flinty in the flashlight beam. Scrawny as he was, there was something in his quiet anger that made him seem extremely dangerous, a panther held back by a thin cord of steel wire.

Even armed, Mask One and Two treated him as if they knew it, too. Not once did they stand within Elmer's reach.

When we were all ashore on the tiny island, Elmer finally spoke. "I ain't one to bother reporting small transgressions, being as I bin known to commit one or two myself. And so far, this here ain't serious. Not yet. Gits much worse, though, and I'll be bound by honor to turn you deputies in first chance I get."

Mask Number One snorted. "Deputies? No matter who you or the boy think we might be, you cain't identify us in a court a' law." He tapped his mask as proof. "And be grateful fer that;

otherwise you'd be marked for gator bait, too."

Too? A long fingernail of iced fear sliced into my stomach.

Elmer shook his head. "T'ain't right, involvin' innercent chillren like this."

"Clem shoulda thought a' that afore draggin' 'em in."

Mask Number Two grabbed a lantern from the airboat, lit it, then shouted from our circle of light into the darkness around the shack. "Hey, you two, git out here. This island's too small fer us not to find y'awl."

A new fear filled me, on top of all the others that crowded my stomach for attention. *What if Lisa and Joel already escaped somehow? Or what if Big Ben made a surprise appearance and—*

Joel dropped in front of me, teddy bear and all.

"Aaaack!" How can someone make you so angry and grateful all at the same time? I mean, a normal person would have said something before leaving the branch outlined above in the moonlight.

Lisa, on the other hand, made a much more dignified climb down the tree. "It seemed safest up there, Ricky," she began as soon as her feet were on the ground. "But what and how—"

"Thass 'nuff," Mask Number One cut her short. "We got business ahead."

He spun on me. "Now, boy. Last chance. Tell us where you hid the coin. And don't try that poor excuse 'bout it being in the mail. We waited all day and seen nothing. And it ain't in the post office bags waiting to be sorted, either. 'Nother words, you been lying. Now 'fess up."

Surely, with Elmer here as a witness, they won't do anything crazy now. Maybe it was the best time possible to end my impossible bluff.

"I don't have it," I said finally. "I never did. I only let you believe it was in the mail because I didn't know what you'd do when you found out I had no idea what it was or what it looked like."

A muffled grunt from Mask Number Two. "You're ordering your own funeral, son."

He snapped his fingers and Mask Number One pulled out a roll of gray duct tape, the kind construction workers use to seal the seams of ventilation ducts.

Mask Number Two pushed me up against the lone tree near shore. I stumbled across one of the clay moonshine jugs Joel had found but kept my balance.

Then—at his next words—that fingernail of iced fear became an entire grasping claw.

"When you're taped real nice to this here tree," he said, "and Big Ben comes a-calling, maybe you'll be remembering a touch more."

On a normal night the rough edges of tree bark against my back would have hurt. And on a normal night I would have complained at the tightness of the tape across my chest and arms.

But this—as my churning stomach said too clearly—was not a normal night. Not with the edge of the dark water less than two steps away. Not with the eerie night noises I heard between each of my strained breaths.

"Boy, listen good," Mask Number Two said.

As if I had a choice.

"There's a good reason y'awl been taped to this here tree. And maybe it's not what you figure."

It's not hard to figure at all. He wants an alligator the size of your average rhinoceros to emerge from the water and use its jaws to crush the life out of me.

"No, boy, it ain't gonna be as simple as havin' ol' Big Ben come up and end it all fer you real quick. Iffen it were that simple, we wouldn't 'a wasted three dollars a' tape to fasten y'awl to that tree. We'd 'ave jest left y'awl in a bundle near the shore."

Elmer made a move of protest. Mask Number One lifted the barrel of his shotgun and froze Elmer in position.

Mask Number Two kept talking as if nothing had happened. "See, the way 'tis now, there ain't no way fer Big Ben to haul you away."

I still did not understand.

"Naw," Mask Number Two said as he hung the lantern on a branch above me, "that gator'll come up, see the light, smell a good meal, and try to tear you away from the tree. 'Course, it won't work with you so firmly attached by the tape. Not at first. Maybe he'll git a good grip on your leg and chew it up a bit."

I could not believe what I was finally beginning to understand.

"Then we'll scare 'im away and ask you about the coin. Iffen you don't answer, we'll call Big Ben up again. And he'll be hungry and mad and remembering what kinda tender morsel we scared him from. Maybe he'll git ahold a' the same leg. Maybe he'll git your foot. Or an arm. We'll let him tug a bit more, then scare him away and ask you again about the coin."

Mask Number Two shrugged. "By the fifth or sixth return trip, Big Ben'll 'ave had most of y'awl. One or two bites at a time."

I was almost glad for the patch of tape that covered my mouth. Without it, I would have screamed in terror.

" 'Tain't human!" Elmer said with gritted teeth. "Torturing a boy like that!"

Mask Number One turned on him slowly. "Figure buckshot'll shut yo' mouth?"

Mask Number Two moved to the water, reached palm down, and slapped six times.

CHAPTER 26

Beneath the light of the lantern, I felt alone on a stage far removed from the world.

How long in real time did it take for the water at the shore's edge to swell at the approach of a monster? I didn't know; I was beyond understanding seconds or minutes.

In that eternity of waiting, I saw over and over again how Big Ben had first attacked the meat left for him on land. In my mind I saw the blackness of surging water becoming the glistening blackness of an alligator's snout. Then the wicked broad head. Cold, flat eyes. And gleaming teeth that had slashed at the chunk of meat like the crack of a whip.

So when Big Ben finally did appear, for a moment I didn't know if it really was him or just the picture in my mind.

Then I heard the water drip from his thick hide, and a splash as he used his gigantic tail to push onto land, and I knew this was no replay in my mind. Big Ben had arrived. Like a fish brought to the surface of water that suddenly understands the danger of the hook, I fought and squirmed against the unyielding tape that held me to the tree, wrestling hard enough that the tape edges cut through my skin.

Insane, the thoughts that struggle for dominance in a situation like that. Part of my mind idled with a horrid curiosity. *What will the first slash of his jaws feel like? Will I pass out from shock?*

Another part of my mind recorded everything about the

alligator, as if a camcorder were taping this for later use. I heard the grunt of the gator and the swish of his upper body clearing the top of the grass. I smelled, or maybe imagined I smelled, stale rotten air from his open mouth.

Yet another part of my mind kept telling me not to give my captors the satisfaction of knowing how terrified I was. So I didn't scream into the tape over my mouth, I didn't flail my legs, and I stopped my useless fight against the tape.

That may be what saved my life, holding completely still.

The alligator paused, as if puzzled. Suddenly I wasn't a struggling living supper in his eyes but an unusual growth on the tree.

It was enough of a pause for Lisa to surprise all of us.

Both our captors were concentrating so hard on preventing Elmer from doing anything that they had ignored Joel and Lisa.

The gator took a halting step forward and opened his mouth wide just as Lisa flew into the circle of light beneath the lantern and yelled her best karate scream.

From there, everything became a tangled blur.

The gator roared and lurched ahead.

Lisa stooped and grabbed the nearest weapon—the clay moonshine jug that was on the ground near my feet.

The gator roared again.

Lisa lifted the jug and smashed it downward and ahead at the gator in a two-handed throw. The jug bounced off the gator's bottom teeth and then inward as those massive jaws snapped shut in fury.

Her timing—accidental or not—was perfect.

Another roar of rage, and as the jaws flashed open again, I saw that the ancient clay of the jug had shattered into dozens of shards, each piece of hardened clay razor-sharp. The gator bellowed and thrashed as if in a giant vise. His mouth opened and closed as he gnashed against the unseen enemy within.

Then, from the corner of my eye, I caught another movement.

Elmer had taken advantage of the distraction beneath the lantern to dive forward.

He crashed his elbow into the head of the first rubber mask and, in the same motion, plowed headfirst into the stomach of Mask Number Two, grabbing the shotgun with both hands as he continued ahead. Then he spun around and, with that shotgun as a baseball bat, clubbed the other gun loose from Rubber Mask Number One.

It happened that quickly.

Both men disarmed. Elmer in control. The alligator thrashing its way backward into the water. Lisa stunned in disbelief at the results of her unthinking action.

And I still had both legs, both arms, and a little brother ripping the skin from my face as he tried to yank the tape free from my mouth.

Pain never felt so good.

CHAPTER 27

"We was jest runnin' a bluff on the boy," Rubber Mask Number Two said. "We was gonna send the gator back and give the boy another chance to talk."

"I ain't real keen on the kind of poker you decided to play," Elmer said. His shotgun did not waver.

While he guarded both men, Lisa helped Joel remove the rest of the tape.

"Thanks, Lisa," I whispered. "I owe you—"

"You owe me nothing," she said firmly. "I did it for me. Had to find a way to stop those guys so I could get off the island."

Then she grinned. "Besides, the last thing I need is you spending the rest of your life paying me back because you think girls shouldn't have to rescue guys."

Ouch. I hate it when she's right.

Fortunately, Elmer did not give me any time to have to think of a good reply.

"Grab what's left of their tape," he instructed me without taking his eyes off either man. "Sidle round back a' them and strap their wrists real tight. Iffen they don't offer their hands quick, we'll see how much incentive a load a' buckshot'll supply."

It took me five minutes. Not because I was slow, but because I wanted it done right.

No words were exchanged. As I taped, I caught the faint smell of skunk from Mask Number One. And now that the danger was over, I could think of other important things, like how bad Joel still smelled and how terrible it was going to be around him back in civilization.

When I finished, Elmer walked around behind them and pulled their masks free. He stepped around in front of them again and nodded with satisfaction.

"Clovis and Ernie. The slowest pair a' deputies never to catch a gator poacher."

"Deputies?" Lisa blurted.

I nodded. "And their boss is Sheriff Leroy, Clem Pickett's older brother."

"Hang on. That ain't true!" Clovis said. "Sheriff Leroy don't know nothin' 'bout this."

"Then why did I get chased from the police station?" I asked.

Ernie snorted. "I weren't there, but I can guarantee the answer is simple. Anytime a body runs from cops, cops is sure to follow."

I shook my head as I remembered the jail cell and the bruises on the side of Clem's face. "Then why did Sheriff Leroy beat up Clem?"

"Son, you cain't unnerstand how much Leroy still hates and loves his brother. Loves him 'cause love ain't something a body's got control on, and hates him for havin' kilt a man."

Elmer shifted his weight.

Clovis continued quickly. "I mean no disrespect for your dead pappy, Elmer. And none when I say Sheriff Leroy lost his temper a couple days back 'cause Clem tried telling him that Elmer's pappy was still alive. Put Leroy in a real bad temper, and Clem, he jest shut up like he did at the trial."

I persisted. "But why would Sheriff Leroy pretend he never heard of the coin when I first went into the station?"

Clovis shrugged, a painful move with his hands tied, as a grimace on his face showed. "Maybe he don't like to admit the trouble they caused; maybe he don't like to know Clem's involved in more badness, right outta jail up north."

Elmer coughed. It brought Clovis and Ernie to instant attention.

"Don't mean to break into this here interestin' tea party, but then, who all is your boss?"

"We don't know," Clovis said. "I got a letter one day what said if Ernie and me wanted to make a fair sum a' money, jest tie a ribbon on my car antenna. We got curious and put the ribbon up. Next day a letter comes what tells me to look in a certain mailbox, and lookee that, there's a fat envelope what holds some instructions and five hunnerd dollars. Me and Ernie hardly make 'nuff to feed ourselves, let alone our families, so we play along and take the money."

"That's right," Ernie said. "And when he told us to get the kids and find out about the coin, we knew all along we'd let the kids go back home safe. We figured no harm be done."

"But I didn't have the coin," I told him. "I never knew what it was. How'd some unseen boss man decide we had it?"

Ernie shook his head. "Clem keeps to hisself purty good. You was strangers, but he went outta his way to be with you at the airport. We figured there had to be a reason. So did the boss man when he called us in Orlando after we took Clem into custody that day."

"You talked to him on the phone," I said. "You couldn't recognize his voice?"

"He was always a-whispering. That don't give clues. Plus, he always made real careful arrangements to call us. That way we don't have no number to track down."

Lisa spoke. "But how did you find us after the airport? Orlando has tens of thousands of tourists."

Ernie grinned despite his predicament. "We're lawmen. We seen you with Clem and watched the car you got into. 'Tweren't no trouble to figure out your location after we took the plate number a' that fancy limousine. We jest strolled into your hotel room and took a good look for the coin. Since we couldn't find it, we did the next best thing. Took the film from the camera fer developin'. We figured someone's mug shot be on it. Then, to keep it real safe, we squeezed a couple of ex-cons to pretend to be cops. Cain't be us, cause then we wouldn't be able to let you go after. So we told them ex-cons iffen they don't help kidnap you, we'd be findin' ways to send 'em back to jail real quick. With them photos in hand, it was real easy for them to find you in Disney World. Even if the boy looked real dumb in that one shot."

Me in the limo caught in surprise by Ralphy. Hah, hah. But at least now we had an explanation for why Ralphy had taken all those shots with an empty camera.

Elmer coughed again. More instant attention from Ernie and Clovis. "Sounds like a lotta risk for hardly any money."

"No siree," Clovis said. "We weren't gonna hurt no one. We figured iffen we didn't do the kidnapping, someone else would, and they might not care as much. So it'd be better for us to do it. And we was gittin' ten thousand dollars."

Elmer whistled. "Ten thou? Whoever's behind this has got a lot of faith that gettin' my pappy's coin from Clem Pickett would surely lead to Madman Charlie's treasure."

Then Elmer chuckled. "A durn stupid faith. Iffen my pappy couldn't find that treasure by only holdin' one coin, nobody else is gonna."

"Thass the peculiar part," Clovis said. "This boss man tells us to be on the lookout fer *two* coins, when we plainly know the legend 'bout Madman Charlie."

"Two coins? You only asked me about *one* coin," I said.

"Only one to worry about. Son, we growed up here," Ernie replied. "When we was boys, we all knew Leroy's pappy gave him that one coin afore leavin' fer war. We all knew that coin was the one thing Leroy loved most dearly. Leroy never went nowhere without that coin on a chain 'round his neck."

Clovis took his turn. "Which is exactly why we been askin' fer one coin. We know Leroy's got the other. But to the man hisself, we weren't gonna call him wrong, not with his givin' us that much money."

Ernie broke in, and his voice carried a frightened plea. "We decided if Big Ben don't git the whereabouts of the coin from you, then you'd be a-tellin' the truth. We was scheduled to be lettin' you go tomorrow. Honest."

Elmer grunted and, after some consideration, spoke. "I ain't sparklin' white myself when it comes to abiding with the law. And I ain't real particular in my feelings about Sheriff Leroy. But in this here situation, I gotta bring y'awl in and let him make heads or tails a' what to do."

Then Elmer turned to me. "Son, I figure you been on the run all day, what with escapin' here, then gittin' dragged back. We'll bring you and yo' friends into Dade City, let you git rested up some, and make sure y'awl git back to yo' friends tomorrow. That's way more important than fitting the pieces together on a mystery that don't make sense nohow."

I nodded. It sounded good. A real bed. Maybe a warm shower. Decent food. And back to Mike and Ralphy and Amanda.

"One thing, son."

"Yes?"

"Let's make sure that brother a' your'n sets way back in the boat, where the wind'll carry his stink away. He smells even worse'n you."

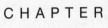 

CHAPTER 28

My brotherly love for Joel lasted exactly seven hours and twelve minutes after our arrival at Mrs. Pickett's house back in Dade City. That's how long I managed to sleep before I rolled over in the double bed we shared and stabbed my rear on his teddy bear.

"Stupid kid," I muttered. Naturally, my yowl of agony hadn't disturbed his sleep for a second.

I rubbed away the pain.

I stopped and looked thoughtfully at the ceiling.

How can a teddy bear stab me?

I reached below the covers and pulled it free to discover that a safety pin had popped loose from one of its legs. Then I remembered—what seemed like a lifetime ago, even though it was only a few days—that Joel had disappeared in the Orlando restaurant to search for a safety pin.

I yawned, tossed the bear on the floor, and received an immediate jab in the ribs from Joel.

He stared at me accusingly.

It figures. I can yelp at three hundred decibels with no effect, but let that soft thud of a teddy bear bouncing on the floor reach his ears and the kid's wide awake.

Then a strange thought jolted me wide awake as I stretched over to reach the teddy bear.

It took less than twenty seconds to confirm my suspicion.

And less than ten minutes for me to reach the sheriff's office.

"Maw took care of y'awl?" Sheriff Leroy asked. His eyes were bleary, and the jowls of his face sagged gray with his obvious fatigue. "Tomater juice bath fer the young'un and lots a' food?"

"Yes, sir," I said. The clock on the wall behind the counter showed 8:05 A.M.

"So what brings y'awl down so early? Checkin' to see if them delinquent deputies is strung up yet?"

I shook my head. "A few questions, sir."

"I'm plain tired, son. And you best be gittin' back to Orlando. It's gonna be a real mess straightenin' all this out."

"Yes, sir." I waited.

He sighed. "Go ahead, son. I kin tell by your face that you ain't leaving until you git some answers."

"The coin your father gave you," I began. "It was important?"

Sheriff Leroy squinted, and his eyes almost disappeared in the fat of his face. "Son, that's right personal."

"I'm sorry, sir. Please let me ask some different questions. Was that coin stolen *before* Elmer Johnson's father was murdered? And why does everyone still think you have it?"

Sheriff Leroy spun on his heels and marched around the counter faster than I would have guessed possible. Within seconds he faced me directly, a huge paw squeezing my shoulder.

"Son," he said in a low and cold voice, "don't be messing with pains and hurts that belong t'others."

I reached into my pocket—a painful move because he still clutched my shoulder—and pulled out a dull gold coin the size of a silver dollar. A tiny hole had been drilled into the top, barely large enough for a necklace chain.

"I found it in my brother's teddy bear, sir. Clem must have hidden it there when he said good-bye to my brother in the airport." I wasn't yet sure if I should tell Sheriff Leroy I had also found the second coin or what I thought that meant.

Sheriff Leroy recognized the first coin instantly. He relaxed his grip on my shoulder, then squeezed tight again, tight enough to make me gasp.

"Fine, smart boy. Y'awl proved the coin was taken. Thass 'nuff now."

I shook my head. "If people knew Clem had *your* coin at the time Elmer Johnson's father was murdered, then at the trial they'd decide it was enough motive for him to kill to get the *other* coin. But maybe back then you decided to keep quiet about your missing coin because if the body was never found, then Clem couldn't be proven guilty."

Sheriff Leroy relaxed his grip and faked disinterest. "This is a borin' story, son. Y'awl best be gittin' on home."

"I think," I said, "it must have been a terrible decision to face, sir. Do you pursue your duty and reveal evidence that would send your brother to jail? Or do you follow the love of a brother and say nothing?"

Sheriff Leroy yawned.

"Except," I persisted, "after you decided to protect Clem, he didn't say a word in his defense during the whole trial. The jury decided that was enough indication of guilt. So you lost both ways. Your younger brother was condemned to jail, and you betrayed your duty."

Finally Sheriff Leroy reacted. He slammed a huge palm on the counter, hard enough to rattle pens and pencils in their trays.

"Git home, boy! Afore I rip your head offen your shoulders."

We stared at each other. Then I said it as quietly as I could.

"What if Clem thought he was protecting *you* from a murder charge? Even if it meant his going to jail in your place?"

"I'm sorry, son," Clem said from behind the bars. "I truly figured no harm could come to y'awl."

We were alone in the cell area.

Clem looked as bowed and tired and bruised as he had when I last saw him sitting as he was now on the edge of the thin mattress.

"I hadn't expected Leroy's deputies to be there in the airport, and there was a tiny rip in the teddy bear for me to push both coins inside, so I took the chance while I was saying good-bye. I knew your brother's name and his hometown and that it was a small town. I figured that was enough to track him down later, when it'd be safe fer me to keep the coins again. I never dreamed the deputies here'd be able to track you down amongst all the tourists."

I explained to Clem how they had managed.

"Bad luck," Clem agreed. "And I'll say it again; I'm truly sorry fer the harm to y'awl."

"We're fine now," I said. Then grinned. "Besides, you owed me one for the caterpillar sandwich on the plane."

His tired grin brought little life to his face, and he said nothing else.

"I'm not here for an apology or explanation, though," I said. "Sheriff Leroy's given me a few minutes to ask you some questions. I said I'd give him your answers only if you decided that would be fine."

Clem shrugged. That movement, however, did not hide the flash of pain to hear his brother's name mentioned.

"You thought your brother, Leroy, killed Elmer Johnson's father," I said.

Clem stared long and hard at me.

"You were the first one at the murder scene, and you found the coin your brother always wore around his neck, the coin everyone knew was the most important object in the world to your brother, the final gift from your father before he went to war. So you kept the coin and told no one, and you assumed Leroy was the murderer."

More tickings of silence.

"When he was there on Moonshiner's Bay to arrest you moments after you left the shack," I said a few moments later, "it convinced you even more. How could he have been there so quickly, unless he had done it himself? So you—"

"It was him an' a couple a' others, slapping handcuffs on me in the rain," Clem croaked. "I ain't never gonna forget how much that hurt. I was jest eighteen, a boy, and my only hero was right there, arrestin' me for something what he done. But I hoped Leroy musta kilt the man in self-defense, and I figured any time he'd explain it so I could go free, and he'd not be charged with murder. And the longer I waited, the more it hurt, until finally I realized it was too late. And by then iffen I accused Leroy nobody'd believe me anyway, so there weren't no sense in makin' it worse, 'specially since it'd break Ma's heart to see her boys turnin' on each other like that. And before I knew it, I was sent up north."

Sadness crossed the giant man's face. "I was jest a confused and scar't boy. It all happened real quick."

He smiled, but the sadness did not leave. "The years in jail 'tweren't nothin' compared to the feelin' that I didn't have a brother no more."

The jangle of keys at the end of the hallway announced that Sheriff Leroy was opening the steel door that separated the cells from the office.

"A month before my sentence was up," Clem said quietly, "Elmer Johnson's pappy visited me in jail. It confused me real good. Iffen he ain't dead, then Leroy didn't murder him. Before I could celebrate, though, Elmer Johnson's pappy explained something else."

The steel door opened and we heard footsteps.

"Ol' Man Johnson said he figured that my brother, Leroy, was one a' the two fellows what forced him to pretend to be dead all these years. That iffen he showed his face here in Dade City, then fatal accidents would happen to his family folks and no one would believe his word against two lawmen. So Ol' Man Johnson asked could I maybe step softly on my return and git this mess straightened out even if Leroy was now sheriff. I came back home with both coins and knowing I still had to keep my mouth shut tighter'n a miser's wallet."

Sheriff Leroy stopped behind me and spoke quietly.

"Clem," he said, "it's about time we started trustin' each other again. Thataway we kin both get the snake of a man what turned us on each other."

Clem and Leroy instructed me to stay in the sheriff's truck. But they weren't specific on how *long* they wanted me to wait. So I gave them five minutes, then stepped out into the already warm Florida morning.

I heard voices long before I saw them. Blake Hotridge and Clem Pickett.

"Backwoods crackers?" Clem was saying as I got closer.

"Backwoods crackers," Blake sneered. "All of you. Leroy. The Johnsons. You tell me you broke out of Leroy's jail? I'm surprised you were smart enough to do that or even figured it out now to come see me. Not that it's going to do you any good."

I dropped to my hands and knees. I crawled to the edge of the path—checking carefully for snakes—then lowered myself to my stomach so that I could peer from beneath an overhanging bush.

I saw immediately why Blake Hotridge spoke with such confidence in the clearing in front of his cabin. He held the same shotgun he'd used against the cottonmouth snake.

"Just a few simple lies," Blake said. He stood at ease, as if he were discussing the weather. "That's all it took. Leroy believed me when I said you stole his coin. Elmer's daddy believed me when I said Leroy was helping me with his fake murder. And you were too dumb to open your mouth."

"Let me git this straight," Clem said. "You tole brother Leroy that I took the coin that Pappy left behind fer him."

Blake shrugged. "Only after I managed to steal it myself. I mentioned I'd seen you leaving his room while he was sleeping and let him suspect the rest. But I'd planned it for a long time. Long before leaving the academy."

"I don't unnerstand," Clem said.

"That doesn't surprise me," Blake snorted. "I'll humor you. I heard rumors about Leroy in the academy. How people thought it was ironic that the grandson of a famous moonshiner would become a Fed. I asked Leroy. He said he never believed in the treasure and figured his life was his own to run as he pleased. So I snuck a look at the old files on the case and decided I *did* believe in Madman Charlie and his long-hidden fortune. Enough belief to make friends with Leroy and get us an assignment down here to reopen the case and put pressure on the Johnsons."

"You planned this from the beginnin'?" asked Clem.

"Dumb cracker. Of course I did. All I needed was to get rid of Elmer Johnson's father on one side, Leroy on the other, and get both their coins. That would give me the time and opportunity to hunt until I found the fortune. So I waited months to steal Leroy's, then traced its markings before leaving it behind at the fake murder scene."

A blade of grass tickled my chin. The discomfort was easy to ignore.

"And Johnson was easy," Blake explained. "All I had to do was catch him poaching an alligator. Then I gave him two choices. He could go to jail and be sure that while he was in jail, every one of his children would have fatal accidents. Or he could give me his coin, go along with the fake murder, and disappear until I left the county."

" 'Tain't right," Clem protested. "He's been waiting all these years."

Blake frowned. "Don't think I'm happy taking this long to find Madman Charlie's millions. Especially after I discovered the coin Johnson gave me two days later—the other half to finding the treasure—was a fake. And me with no way of tracking him down to get the real one."

"The blood in the shack the day of his pretend murder," Clem said. "If it weren't from Ol' Man Johnson, how'd you expect people to believe a body'd been murdered?"

"Simpleton," Blake said. "Who would be in charge of the investigation and paper work but the FBI man on the scene? If *I* didn't want to discover it was only chicken blood, it wouldn't get discovered. The drag marks to the water were easy enough to make. I'd already traced the markings on the coin I'd stolen from Leroy, so all I had to do was leave Johnson's wallet and knife and Leroy's coin behind. That would take care of my second problem, how to get rid of your brother. Everybody knew Leroy treasured that coin above everything because it was a keepsake from his father, who died in the war. To find the coin at the murder scene would frame him perfectly, especially because everybody would think he'd killed Johnson to get the other coin."

Clem scratched his head, looking puzzled.

I wanted to scratch my own throat at the itchiness that grew but didn't dare. Any movement might attract attention.

"But I'm the one who got took on the island that day," Clem said.

Blake shrugged. "Bad luck on your part. Remember the message your mother got?"

Clem nodded. "That I was supposed to meet Ol' Man Johnson out at Moonshiner's Bay at exactly 8 P.M."

Blake laughed. "She got it wrong. I had called her and told her that *Leroy* was supposed to meet Ol' Man Johnson out there. I was furious to discover she'd made a mistake. By then it was too late. The former sheriff—before Leroy quit the bureau and took over—had already gotten my next phone call, the one tipping him to the possibility of trouble out there between a Pickett and a Johnson because of an eight o'clock meeting. I never dreamed the sheriff would call Leroy to see if it was true and that both of them would decide to check it out and find *you* there."

His laugh grew even more nasty. "But things worked out, didn't they? You took the blame because you thought finding Leroy's coin meant he was the murderer. And Leroy just gave up on being a good lawman because he thought you'd done it. He didn't care about anything and settled for becoming a local sheriff later on. Me? I stayed around and have been looking for the treasure ever since. Why else would I have this cabin so close to the island?"

"But even if I weren't there," Clem said, "there weren't nothing to stop Johnson from coming back and ruinin' your frame-up."

"Sure was." Blake grinned. "He was on a ship headed to South America, ticket courtesy of me. I'm not stupid. Unlike you."

"Me?" Clem asked.

"You don't think I'd be telling you all this if I planned to let you live, do you?"

Clem dropped his dumb country boy act and his voice became like flint against flint. "And y'awl don't think I'd be here alone?" He looked over Blake's shoulder. "Did he say enough yet, Leroy?"

"Nice try," Blake sneered.

His sneer changed to surprise at the audible click of a gun's hammer being drawn back.

"It's enough confession fer me," Leroy said as he stepped out from beside the cabin. "Drop it, Blake. Now!"

Blake set the gun down slowly. That's when I stood up and screamed and began to beat my body frantically.

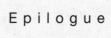

Epilogue

"You know," Mike said halfway through my story, "the only reason I believe any of this so far is that we're in Dade City and you're lying here in a hospital bed."

"Yeah," Ralphy added. "For two days, all of us on both ends—Orlando and Jamesville—thought you were safe at the other. And you better be glad your parents aren't in Florida yet. They promised to skin you alive for not calling the instant you got out of the swamp area."

I moaned. "Don't use that word."

"Skin?"

I moaned again.

Mike clucked. "The only guy in the world smart enough to help Clem and Leroy clue in on Blake Hotridge. And the only guy in the world dumb enough to belly his way right on top of a nest of fire ants."

I let my moan grow. Not that it gained me sympathy.

"Did you know fire ants were once native only to South America?" Ralphy asked. "But they were introduced by accident to Florida and are now considered one of the most vicious insects in the United States. Unlike bees, they can sting over and over again and—"

"Thanks, encyclopedia brain."

I renewed my groaning, and they respected my agony for at least another ten seconds before starting again.

"You haven't told us," Mike said. "How did Clem and Leroy decide Blake Hotridge was behind all of this?"

I rubbed more calamine lotion on my body before explaining how easy it had been once the two of them finally exchanged stories. Blake had always thought he would be long gone with the money before Clem got out of jail, so he hadn't worried too much. In fact, it was only the lie to Old Man Johnson about having help from Leroy that had kept Clem silent awhile longer.

Discovering it was Blake had come down to asking questions. Who suggested to Sheriff Leroy that Clem should be arrested again, this time by coming up with false charges on a few old crimes that had never been solved? Who had told Sheriff Leroy he suspected Clem had stolen his coin? Who lived near enough to Moonshiner's Bay to be able to train an alligator from birth to come to shore at six slaps on the water?

Once Blake Hotridge's name came up, it made sense why he had retired so early and stayed in the area. And how he had "happened" to rescue me from the snake when instead—as he admitted later—he was following me around to make sure I didn't get hurt or killed before the coin was found. It also made sense that—once he found me near the swamp—he had decided to let Clem, in the Dade City Jail, see me so that Clem would know we'd really been kidnapped and would later be pressured into telling where he had placed the coins.

How had Blake been able to know so certainly that Clem had both coins when he left prison? Sheriff Leroy made some calls and discovered that Blake had used his former FBI connections to get some "courtesy information" about Clem's possessions as he was checked out of Sing Sing prison. With that knowledge, Blake had made anonymous arrangements so that the deputies would arrest Clem right off the airplane and nab the coins.

Looking back, Blake had taken a lot of desperate steps. Yes, it would have been a long shot for everything to work out for him. But he had spent all that time around Moonshiner's Bay trying to find the rumored treasure and wasn't about to quit.

It was our misfortune to get in the way of his desperation. Or, as I explained, it was something a person should learn to expect with a brother like Joel.

Of course, Joel does have his good points. Like his knack for finding things of value that others overlook.

Because there was one thing I had told no one until Leroy and Clem were back in the sheriff's office to reunite the two coins that Madman Charlie had designed so many years ago. The combined markings on the coins showed the outlines of a single tree, and it was then I realized exactly what Joel had found.

But we wouldn't know the truth of my guess for at least another half hour.

"The patient is fine," Lisa said with a huge grin as she stepped into my hospital room, "and has given birth to handfuls of sparkling diamonds."

Mike and Ralphy and I applauded.

Then she marched right to the side of my bed and kissed me on the cheek.

"Ho, ho!" Mike chortled. "I didn't think his skin could get any redder."

"Wait till I'm out of here," I warned Mike. "You'll be—"

"Mike," Lisa said, "I think it was sweet of Ricky to insist on making a deal for Big Ben's life before telling anyone his theory. Even if it was as crazy as anything he's imagined before."

"Hey!" I said. "It was Elmer Johnson who said Madman Charlie told his kids that there would be more money than 'twinkling stars.' It was Joel who found that stupid jug up there in the branches when you guys were hiding alone on the island. And it was you who made that stupid alligator chomp down on the jug. Can I help it if I was the one who was so close to Big Ben that I saw right in his mouth when it happened?"

I shuddered at the memory. But when I closed my eyes, it was there again, the split-second view of tiny rocks, brighter in the lantern light than any broken clay should ever be.

Mike groaned. "Say that again, Lisa. Ricky was right about the diamonds in the alligator? We'll never hear the end of this."

Before I could gloat, Clem Pickett walked into the room. Amanda stepped in behind him, holding Joel's hand.

"Son, we made you a promise, and we aim to keep it. The veterinarian says Big Ben'll be fine in a couple of days. We jest need to keep him in an outside pen near water till that slit in his belly heals. Then we'll set him free."

He squinted at me. "It beats all, though, you insistin' we don't kill the critter."

I shrugged, painful as it was with the sheets rubbing against my inflamed skin. I think it was that I felt something in common with Big Ben. I'd survived the entire craziness. I guess I wanted him to do the same.

It was just hard to picture a fifteen-foot alligator bound and stretched unconscious across a couple of surgery tables as a vet and assistants worked on searching his stomach for the diamonds.

"Tell me," I said to Clem, "was Big Ben hard to find and catch?"

Clem started laughing. He laughed so hard that within minutes all of us were laughing with him, even though we didn't know why.

He finally stopped and wheezed for breath.

"Hard to catch, son? Think about it. That gator swallowed everything. Diamonds, chunks of clay, and an entire jug of moonshine what's been sitting on the island for nigh upon forty years. Big Ben was sleeping like a baby on dry land in the middle a' daylight. Weren't nothing we could do to wake the critter."

Clem's face crinkled into softness. "Elmer's got hisself his pappy back soon's I git word to Ol' Man Johnson that it's clear now. Blake Hotridge ain't gonna cause no fatal accidents to no one."

Clem fumbled with his hands, awkward now as he struggled for words. They finally came, slow and halting. "And I got me back a brother."

We pretended not to see the single tear that tracked his left cheek.

Clem then shrugged shyly and patted Joel on the head as a farewell gesture. The room seemed much emptier after the big man left.

When all the rest of my visitors left the room and after the nurse had drawn the shades to let me suffer in silence and darkness and gratitude of being alive, I began to compose my school essay on how I spent my summer holiday:

"I knew it was going to be trouble when I bashed a six-foot-six ex-con across the face and forced him to eat half a caterpillar. . . ."

Later I smiled and pretended to be asleep when Joel crept back into the room and held my hand.

The Most Fun You Can Have
Reading!

Around the World With Christian Heroes!

Travel the globe and go back through time with the TRAILBLAZER BOOKS! Whatever country or time interests you most, chances are there's a TRAILBLAZER BOOK about it. Learn about Christian heroes— their dangerous and exciting lives— through the eyes of a boy or girl about your age.

TRAILBLAZER BOOKS
by Dave and Neta Jackson

Madcap Mysteries With a Message!

Strange things are afoot in the town of Midvale, and Bloodhounds, Inc. is on the case. A detective agency formed by Sean and Melissa Hunter, along with their slobbery bloodhound, Slobs, Bloodhounds, Inc. finds itself on the trail of ghosts, UFOs, and other strange and seemingly supernatural things. With a deep trust in God's protection and some keen investigating, the two teens help bring the bright light of truth into some scary places.

BLOODHOUNDS, INC. by Bill Myers

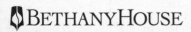